<u>PRAISE FOR PETE RISLEY</u>

"Risley's cold but soul-searing novel snatched my attention irrevocably from the opening passage. Its dark frights are as scary as the things on offer in good horror fiction. In a way good noir and good horror aren't that far removed from each other in spirit. Nowhere is this better illustrated than in Rabid Child. The humans are the horror but this book is honestly frightening."

—Kristofer Todd Upjohn, author of
Jess Franco: The World's Most Dangerous Filmmaker

"Murder-minded singer and author Nick Cave has nothing on Pete Risley. Risley's debut novel, *Rabid Child,* reads like the unholy offspring of Brian Evenson and Erskine Caldwell, of Thom Metzger and Jim Thompson, of Tim Burton and William Lindsay Gresham. It's *Carnival of Souls* re-filmed for the twenty-first century, possessing an air of creepy menace and swampedelic grimness that is simultaneously hip and eternal, off-putting and seductive, melancholy and hilarious. Desmond Cray, our perverted anti-hero, is no match for his demented foster sister, uber-slut Tracy Honnecker. Their conjoined and separate trails of lust and destruction through their town—*Peyton Place* via The Book of Revelation—will leave you shaking your head in grinning disbelief."

—Paul Di Filippo, author of
A Mouthful of Tongues a

GIRL OF PREY

PETE RISLEY

For Denny Hammond

1

RONI AT THE LIMBO

Veronica Savinio, known as Roni, sat alone and chain-smoking in a booth at the Limbo, a dumpy bar her asshole husband, Shannon, frequented, waiting for him to show up to take her home after she'd worked late at her job at the Mirror, a nearby movie theater.

"No problem, just walk over to the Limbo," he'd said earlier that evening. "I'll be back there around midnight." He and Dewey had some "errands to run," he'd said, that had to do with "a job," and wanted her to meet him at the bar after work since she didn't want to hang around at the theater longer than she had to. "Okay, but be there right at midnight," she'd insisted, and he'd said sure. She herself wouldn't be there until about 12:15, but he was always late anyway. It was now quarter to one, and no Shannon. Plus, it was the first night of her boss Hobie's beloved Halloween marathon, which she'd had to listen to him obsess over for the last four months, and she'd been working since ten in the morning with first Hobie and later a mob of partying kids driving her nuts, and was totally frazzled.

It was not the first time Shannon had done shit like this to her. Why did she put up with it? Why, in fact, had she married the fuckwad in the first place, when even her kooky friend Clare had read her the handwriting on the wall right from the start? Fucking thirty-four years old already and here she was, married to a total fucking waste of skin and working a shit job in Nowhere, Ohio.

The Limbo, full name Harvey's Limbo Lounge according to the ancient and dingy Pepsi sign outside, was run not by a Harvey but by an old, cranky hilljack named Fred, who at present was sitting back behind the bar with his arms folded, craning his neck and staring crazy-eyed through farmer's glasses at a pastel-suited televangelist on the TV perched high up on the wall above the bar. Then there was Heather, the barmaid, a short and pudgy bottle-blonde who spoke in an affected little-girl voice, giggled constantly and flirted with all the male customers, no matter how old, grizzled and soused they were. She now minced about in front of a befuddled-looking fat guy at the bar with a sparse beard and a hank of graying ponytail sticking out of the back of his John Deere cap.

Most of the regular Limbo patrons were lowlife drunks, some of whom Shannon had known since kindergarten here on the seedy west side of Stankerton. Veronica was from a suburb of Buffalo, New York, not a particularly affluent one, but way better than this flyover shithole, which she saw as a kind of urbanized version of *Green Acres*. *Green Acres* with pot, heroin, meth and oceans of beer.

There were only six other customers present, all familiar except the Deere cap guy, though she didn't remember their names: two ancient ones at a booth hunched close together talking into each other's faces, and two younger and even geekier-looking ones at the battered Ms. Pac-Man machine, pressing buttons with delighted expressions and guffawing when something surprised them on the screen. Most charming of all was Jaime Tales, in his early twenties, the oldest surviving male member of the locally notorious Tales family, sitting at the near end of the bar chewing his lips and darting an occasional lizard-like glance Roni's way.

She checked her reflection in the wavy sides of the small silver jukebox in her booth. Her mark, as she thought of it—the hated dark plum-wine stain that lay beside, over and just beneath her left eye—looked huge, bloated. She knew, in the box's swirled curves, it was hard to tell how much of what she didn't like seeing was funny-mirror effect and how much was really the way it looked. The mark wasn't supposed to change shape or size, and nearly everyone had always told her it didn't. Clare Hardwick, in fact, was the only one who agreed it sometimes blossomed and shifted, perhaps with Roni's moods, or her spiritual state, or even as an omen of forthcoming events. Clare might have been looney tunes in some ways, but Roni was certain the mark did go through changes and was grateful someone else acknowledged it, even if it was a person who aspired to be abducted by UFO aliens. Though she feared the mark might someday alter so radically everyone would agree.

She was also annoyed to see the jukebox-mirror made her chin look like it was doubling. It looked almost like Heather's. But that, she was pretty sure, was just more distortion. She'd been trying to lose weight lately, but the slight sag under her chin wouldn't go away. Maybe, she worried, her whole face was getting droopy because of aging, and that's why the mark was changing as well.

She looked away, lit another cigarette. She probably should have stayed at the theater, but if she had, Hobie would have found some reason why she had to stay longer. And then there was Benny, Hobie's recently discarded boyfriend, who kept wanting her to listen as he poured his broken heart out to her. Anyway, she was just about pissed off enough to order a beer—a light beer, anyway—but she'd have to ask Heather for it. Shannon might have some of that rancid Mexican beer he liked left in the fridge at home, she wasn't sure. If so, that would do.

She might as well go home, she thought. He obviously wasn't going to show up. She could walk, it was only about eight or nine blocks. It was fucking one a.m., and she'd probably get raped and murdered by the Westside Slasher on the way, but, fuck it. That would beat sitting here like a pitiful sap, a fucking Jerry Springer loyal white trash cheated-on housewife.

"Hey, can we change the channel?" said one of the two barflies playing Ms. Pac-Man to Heather, about five seconds after Fred rose from his chair and strode into the kitchen.

"He'll just change it back when he comes back," said Heather.

"Is he comin' right back?"

"Probably. What you want to change it to?" This, Roni gathered, would provide an opportunity for Heather to stand on Fred's chair and sway her big butt right in the face of the bozo with the John Deere cap. Indeed, Heather scooted the chair over and climbed up, wiggling it. Jeez, talk about broad in the beam, girl.

3

"We wanted to see if there was anything on the news about that new victim of the Westside Slasher dude," explained the other barfly playing Ms. Pac-Man.

"It's not a new one, is it?" asked his companion. "Thought it was an old one."

"I think it's an old victim they just found out about," said the guy in the Deere cap, turning on his stool to glance at the others. He didn't seem too interested in Heather's huge ass.

"They're saying now he cuts their fuckin' hearts out," said one of the elderly barflies.

"That's the rumor," said the Pac-Man player.

Roni hadn't heard this before. She exchanged a glance with Heather. "Whaaaa-aat?" said Heather, mouth gaping like a guppy's.

"The Westside Slasher, cuts those girlses' hearts out. Said on the radio."

"Said it's a rumor," his buddy pointed out.

"No way!" said Heather. "Their hearts out?"

"Whoa," said Deere cap. "Sick puppy."

The geeks both nodded. "That's what they're sayin'."

"Omigod, that is so gross!" said Heather. She sounded delighted. "Cuts their hearts out! With what?"

"I dunno. Knife, I guess," said Deere cap. One of the geeks laughed, earning a scowl from Deere cap.

"Ooooo! That just gives me cold chills all over!" She ran her hands up and down her plump arms. "He cuts out their hearts!"

"That's not all," said the other geek. "They're saying he lops their titties off first. Gotta do that to get to the heart, I guess."

"Oh, I dunno, seems like you could get up under there if you knew what you were doin'," said his buddy.

"Well, whatever. 'Course, it's s'posed to be just a rumor, but you know, that's what they always say when they don't want to admit stuff, the police and all."

"What does he do with their hearts and their titties?" said Heather.

"Eats 'em," said Deere cap, grinning.

Heather shrieked. "*He does not!* Does he?"

"Them titties, that's some good eatin'!" His mouth hung open as he chortled. Roni cringed, watching.

"How do you know? You had some of 'em?" said Heather, posed with hands on hips.

"Naw, I'm just doggin' ya."

4

"Oh, don't you start!" said Heather, slapping playfully at him. "You'll about scare me into a conniption. He cuts their hearts out and their titties off! Goodness gracious," she said, rolling her eyes. "Jesus Lord!"

Jesus indeed, thought Roni. Hearts and breasts. She hadn't heard that one. Probably wasn't true. Sounded like scenes from one of the stupid movies at the marathon.

But the whole thing was creepy enough, all right. There'd already been four girls killed over the last few months, and the local media had generated a lot of interest in the case. Even Jaime Tales seemed to become somewhat alert to hear the subject come up, sitting up in his seat and looking from face to face as the barflies spoke.

If this were true about the Slasher cutting hearts out, Roni thought it would probably make the national news before long. Well, that should put the old town on the map. And here she was, probably going to have to walk home, thanks to her shithead hubby. Sweet.

Heather, standing on the chair and swaying, reached up, clunked the TV's knob and stopped at a channel with soundtrack music going that indicated a moment of high drama. On the screen, a leggy girl in cutoffs ran through a night-lit field of gravestones, a terrified look on her face, her long blonde hair streaming behind her. In pursuit came a chubby overalled man brandishing a pitchfork, laughing maniacally, a split-faced grin on his hog-ugly face. The girl suddenly fell forward into what turned out to be an open grave. The camera closed in on her. Looking around, she found herself lying on a decayed corpse in a suit and tie, its mottled skull-like face bearing a grin like that of her pursuer. As she screamed, rolling over and thrashing wildly so her blouse tore open, revealing large breasts in a low-cut bra, the corpse's arms wrapped around her in a seeming embrace. A knot of worms emerged from his empty eye sockets and squirmed apart across his face unto hers, as her own eyes rolled madly.

Heather gave a yelp, turning up the volume.

"Is that the news? Looks like a movie," said one of the geeks.

The man in overalls looked down on the girl, grinning with delight, and seemed about to hurl the pitchfork into the grave when a spotlight fell upon him, accompanied by a high-pitched whirring-and-beeping sound. His expression went blank, and he dropped the pitchfork at his feet just as he began to levitate straight upward into the beam.

"Where's he goin'?" said Deere Cap.

5

"It's just a movie. That's Chiller," said a geek.

"I was gonna say." Deere Cap lifted his glass, downed his beer.

"Oh," said Heather. She sounded disappointed.

In confirmation, the screen went black and the words "Chiller Theatre" rose up in spookily wavering letters. An unseen announcer said, "All right, good groovers, we're watching *Scream of the Ghoul*, also known as *7 Masks of the Faceless Ripper*, 1972, starring Robert Castle, Dominique Saban and Adriana Tori. Don't know those players, but definitely an interesting flick. Stay tuned, we'll be right back after these important messages." A too-familiar replacement window commercial began.

Great, thought Roni, *7 Masks is one of the movies we're showing at the marathon*. Unlike all these dipshits around here, including her husband, she had no use for this kind of crap, but she recalled the title from the bill.

Fred stepped back into the room, wiping his hands on a towel. "What you doin' with my TV? Put Dr. Landfrey back on there."

"Omigod, Fred, did you hear about how those girls the Westside Strangler kilt got their—"

"Yes, I heard you. Quit takin' the Lord's name in vain."

Heather sighed, climbed up again and turned the knob. The screen showed an elderly bespectacled man in a suit and tie, white hair in nearly a pompadour, seated and with his hands clasped together, wearing a fixed smile that puffed his cheeks up like dinner buns. He was, of course, Dr. Trumpeter Landfrey, a popular evangelist with his own cable TV network. His show was apparently on all day, seemed like whenever you were changing channels on TV, he'd be on.

"There he is," said Heather, moping, leaning on the bar, cheek on fist. The customers shrugged and looked away from the TV while Fred moved the chair back to its proper spot, sat down and leaned back, folding his arms and giving the good doctor his full attention.

"Friends," said Dr. Landfrey, speaking in a deep, dramatic voice that seemed it should have been coming out of a wholly different face, "we hear a great deal these days about the ghastly crime of rape, the unspeakably vile, violent violation of our young women . . ."

"He's talkin' about it too," said Deere Cap.

"Police tell us that statistics show the number of these outrages reported in our fair country is ever on the rise, year after year. The so-called feminist organizations allege that even more such crimes, a huge number, go unreported every year, so the claim is made that this

6

problem is greatly worse than our rightful authorities tell us.

"These feminist groups place the blame for the worsening problem on pornography, which indeed overstimulates weak and immoral men. But the feminists say it also encourages all men—every man in the world, these angry Marxist-influenced ladies allege—to see man's traditional helpmate, the woman—every woman—as what they call a sex object. That is, not a person but only a thing to serve as a vessel for lustful contemplation and all that may follow in man's blighted and benighted course." Landfrey hunched down and pressed his lips into a thin, abbreviated line.

"Pornography, we Christians know well, is a heinous menace to the moral fabric of our society." He leaned in closer, folded his hands, shaking his head. "But friends, doesn't good old-fashioned common sense tell us there's a close connection between the repulsive and inescapable presence of pornography in our supposedly enlightened secular world, and the plain fact that so many of our young females today choose to dress in the manner of what in our forefathers' time were termed common harlots, and further, to conduct themselves as if . . ."

"Naw, I guess he's off on something else," said Deere Cap.

". . . for as the Bible teaches in the Book of Proverbs, a loose woman does not take heed to the path of life, her ways wander, and she does not know it, as her feet go down to death . . ."

As the old coot rattled on, he was replaced on the screen by images of angular young fashion models sashaying down runways in strange skimpy outfits. The distant wail of a police siren rose in the background as the scene shifted to grainy images of a young woman lying face-up on the ground, apparently by the side of a road, her clothing disarranged and a superimposed black rectangle covering her eyes.

That's right, cocksucker, thought Roni. *First make all women out to be objects, tell them they're worthless if they're not, then blame them for getting raped and murdered because of how they dress. Fucker. Typical.* Her rising fury made the evil old bastard's further words an aural fog as she stabbed out another half-smoked cigarette.

Fred and the John Deere guy were both nodding in syncopation to Landfrey's sage words. *Fucking redneck morons.*

"That don't justify it, the way girls dress," said Heather, hands posed cutely on her hips, putting on a show as usual.

"He didn't say it justified it," said Fred, "what he's sayin' is that

that's the reason these things happen so much these days. It's the moral decline all over. Moral relativism."

Heather turned and her eyes met Roni's and held for a long moment. She called out loudly, "Ron, honey, did you need anything?"

All heads turned her way. Jaime whirled on his seat, his eyes widening unnervingly.

"No," she said.

"You waitin' on Shannon, hon?" called Heather, seemingly louder than before. *Fuck you, bitch*, thought Roni, seething.

"Don't yell across the room, go on over there. S'posed to be a waitress," said Fred, not looking away from the TV screen.

Heather pouted, jumped up and pranced around from behind the bar, approaching, still speaking at stage volume as she did. "You want a beer or anything, hon? A light beer?"

Light beer. "No, I'm fine. I'm fine. Really." She set her teeth together and smiled at Heather for the briefest moment, then looked away. *Come near me and I'll rip your lungs out, fat little slutbag.*

"Okay, hon, you just let me know," said Heather. "He'll be here, he's just runnin' late probably." She turned and sauntered back to the bar.

To temper her aggravation, Roni thought of an anecdote Heather's sometime friend, Krystal Horsley, told her three or four years ago, one that Krystal claimed Heather had tearfully confided in her. Heather was then shacking up with Bud Junior Tales, Jaime's big and mean older brother. Heather's complaint was that Bud Junior's new-found favorite way of popping off was to bend her over the kitchen table and to place a copy of Hustler's *Barely Legal* open to a compelling photo layout on poor Heather's wide, desk-like back. He'd then pump her plump little jism-jar from behind while looking at the magazine for inspiration, leafing through the pages as he went.

Heather had made Krystal swear on a probably imaginary Bible not to ever tell anyone, but during one of the episodes when Krystal and she were feuding, guess what? Krystal went around and related the juicy tale to a few select girls in the neighborhood, including Roni, swearing each one to silence as well, but without citing the Bible. Later, when Heather and Krystal became friends again, temporarily anyway, Krystal claimed repentantly that she had just made the whole thing up, but to Roni it bore the ring of truth. Last she heard, Krystal was doing a stint in the workhouse for shoplifting, though she was likely out by now.

She lit up a fresh cigarette. Fuck yes, it was true, obviously. Bent over a table with a skin magazine open on her back, getting porked. What a sweet scene to contemplate. Bud Junior had since died in a one-car accident in which he drove his pickup into a stone quarry pool and drowned, under the influence of enough crank to give an elephant a stroke. Then came the demise of the eldest brother, Marlon Tales, who'd shot himself in the face with a pistol, twice—first accidentally, and after two months of sucking pablum through a straw, on purpose. That left only creepy retard Jaime among the brothers, whom even Heather didn't consider an eligible bachelor.

She smiled at her thoughts, exhaling smoke, and glanced over at Heather, who was mopping the bar, looking a bit blue. The John Deere guy, she noticed, was gone from the bar. He might have left, or maybe just went into the men's room. Perhaps he hadn't witnessed Heather's performance just now, disappointing her.

No way was Roni going to order a beer after that "light beer" comment. If she wanted one, she'd definitely have to go home. And she'd have to walk. Yet still she sat there, reluctant to go. All at once she felt like weeping and, at that, was furious again. *Son of a fucking bitch, Shannon, asshole fuckhead loser, where are you? Out driving around with Dewey in Todd Dewolf's fucking Hearsemobile. Shannon and Dewey and fucking Hobie Lautenschlager and all these other jerkoffs around here, with their dipshit Z movies and brain-battering heavy metal music . . .*

She heard the door open, looked up. No, it wasn't him.

Three kids came in, strangers, and quite out of place. Two were guys, both wearing leather jackets and jeans, one with wheat-colored dreadlocks, and the other with a spiky blond punk do. The third was a girl, with sticky, dyed-black hair, straight and shoulder-length, wearing a tight, low-cut black mini-dress with net hose: Morticia, from the hips up.

"Omigod, what a total hole," said the girl, looking around her. All three wore chalk-white face paint with dark eyeshadow and mascara, making them look something like raccoons. Strays from the crowd at the marathon, probably. Everybody but Fred turned to watch as they approached the bar.

"Can I help you?" said Heather, interested.

"S'up. We're looking for a guy," said the kid with dreads. He sounded like he was imitating the voice of a tough street kid as depicted on TV dramas.

Heather bounced and cocked her head to one side. "Anybody I

know?"

"Guy named Shannon. He said we could find him here, maybe."

Something in Roni's chest tightened. *Oh fuck, he's dealing again.*

"Well, I know more than one Shannon," said Heather, glancing Roni's way. "What's his last name?"

"It's obvious she knows who we mean," said the blond, and Morticia simpered out a kind of laugh.

"Chill, dude," said Dreadlocks. "Chill." Blondie shrugged, Morticia rolled her eyes in classic mall-rat style.

Shannon was back to dealing dope. For a job, he'd said. Yeah, this kind of job. *God, what a scumbag.*

"Why are you looking for this Shannon?" Heather glanced Roni's way again, and Blondie followed her glance.

It's probably just pot, she told herself. But no. It was worse. Ecstasy or some shit.

"We're just trying to hook up with him," said Dreadlocks. "Know where we might find him?"

"What's he look like?" said Heather.

"Kind of a tall stocky guy, might be forty, has like real long brown hair parted in the middle," said Dreadlocks. "Has a goatee, sort of. Wears shades all the time. Smirks a lot."

Fred interrupted: "You kids wanna sit down, show some ID and buy a drink, that's fine, but we can't give out no information about customers here."

"What do you want this Shannon for anyway?" said Heather.

"Just because we do," said Morticia in a sweet, chirpy voice. *Snotty little bitch.*

"I ain't talkin' to hear myself speak," said Fred. "You don't wanna buy a drink, you gonna have to leave."

Heather just wouldn't quit. "But if you wanted to leave a message, we could—"

"No, we sure couldn't!" said Fred. "Now," he pointed with a gnarled finger, "if you three don't have no other business here—"

"Okay, okay, it's cool, we're going." Dreadlocks patted Blondie on the shoulder and, with both hands, turned him toward the door. "It's all right, we'll find him."

"Thanks for everything," said Blondie as they exited, and Morticia said, "God, no shit."

Roni lit up the last cigarette in her pack. Dealing something that these wannabe hipster kids go for. Not just pot. Probably some weird

10

designer drug. Something Clare's husband, Todd Dewolf, might come up with. He was worse than Shannon. At least Clare had sense enough to get away from him.

"Well, they sure left with their tail between their legs," said one of the Ms. Pac-Man geeks. "What were they s'posed to be, zombies?"

"They're Goths," said Heather.

"What? Golf?"

"Goth. It's like horror movie stuff in rock music," said his buddy. "Marilyn Manson, Alice Cooper, like that."

"Alice Cooper, shit, that was back when we was in high school."

"Yeah, but it's all the same shit."

"They might have come from the Halloween thing at the Mirror," said Heather. She called out, "You guys are doing that Halloween show tonight, aren't you, Roni? It just started, right?"

Roni nodded yes, not wanting to speak. Heather kept looking her way, probably wanting to say more. Finish this cigarette and go.

The guy in the Deere cap stepped into the room from the hall in the back. He'd been in the men's room. "What? Did I miss something?"

"No. Yes," said Heather. "Roni, hon, was Shannon supposed to—"

"Girl, be still and mind your own business," said Fred. *Thank you,* thought Roni. Heather clammed up and moved down to the far end of the bar, away from Fred. After a minute, he went into the back room again without saying more. The TV was showing a commercial for travel to the Holy Land.

"Well, that kinda broke up the monotony," said one of the geeks, and the other smiled and winked. Heather sat down in Fred's chair, scowling, glancing over at Roni again. Jaime was staring out the window fiercely, unmoving, as the sound came of a car door slamming, an engine starting up.

Shannon had been driving that stupid Todd Dewolf car for how long now? Whatever the drug was, it was Todd coming up with it. Again.

She found she was looking at her wedding ring. She tried to turn it on her finger, but it was stuck. She really was getting fat.

"They gone yet, Jaime?" said one of the geeks. He and the others laughed. Jaime didn't respond, but turned and stared at her again. *Jesus, take a picture.* It occurred to her all at once that it might be her mark everybody was looking at, noticing how it was bigger than

11

before.

Heather leaned forward and spoke something to John Deere, whispering, going on and on. He listened, nodding, and both of them looked over at her together. More whispering, but the guy shook his head, like maybe he didn't want to hear more gossip. Heather shrugged, stepped into the back room.

Enough, can't stand it. Roni stood, grabbed up her bag, and stepped quickly to the door to get out while Heather was out of the room and couldn't call out, "Oh, you leavin', hon?" She felt everyone's eyes on her, but wasn't going to look back.

The outside cold came briskly through the door when she pulled it open, but at least it was fresh. She hated walking home in this shitty neighborhood even in daytime. Streets without sidewalks, no decent streetlights, and cars whizzing past her, maybe those guys from the bar, maybe the Slasher himself. She would walk fast.

Cutting their hearts out. The mark, getting way worse, she knew it really was. Getting fat. And Shannon, dealing again. Fuck him. She pulled her coat together at her throat and hurried, tears brought on first by the cold, soon flooding her eyes and blurring what lights there were as she stepped hard, flooded with despair.

2

SHANNON AND DEWEY ON THE ROAD

Dewey handed the joint over and decided to ask, "So, did Roni get a ride home after all?"

"Whaddaya mean?" said Shannon, keeping his eyes on the road while he took a hit.

"From the movie theater."

"Oh, shit, you're right. We were supposed to go back and get her at the Limbo. Shit." Shannon put out the remaining inch of joint and left it in the ashtray. Dewey didn't want any more anyway, he was feeling pretty stoned, like his head floated somewhere slightly above his inert body. They drove on, quiet.

Dewey broke the silence. "So, where are we going? To pick up Roni?"

"Naw. I'll call her at the Limbo when we get to the club. We gotta meet those kids."

"She's gonna be mad, man."

"She'll get over it."

"We wouldn't be late if Todd had had the shit ready when he said he would."

"Yeah, well, he's distracted."

"I wonder if he's even making it right."

"What, the worm? Sure he is. Customers are very satisfied. Why, you wanna test drive this batch, make sure it's grade A?"

"Not really." Dewey didn't approve of selling it at all, after their own experience of it. He was surprised Todd didn't feel that way about it, too, but maybe that was because he was so burned out about everything now. Anyway, Dewey wasn't going to bring up that whole topic again. They were late because Todd had forgotten about them coming over to pick some up, or so he'd said, and had to finish the process of scraping the miserable stuff out of the frying pan and packaging it up, which took over an hour while Dewey and Shannon sat around watching a fairly gross and repetitious porn video Todd had playing on his VCR.

There was a pause. Cars went by, lights blooming and receding.

"Seriously though," said Dewey, "shouldn't we go get Roni home first? It wouldn't take that long."

"We're already real late to meet the kids. They want their dope."

"Okay, she's your wife."

"Yep, that she is."

There was another lapse in the conversation. Shannon turned off an exit, surprising Dewey.

"Why we going this way?"

"To get to the place where we're going."

"The Morgue isn't this way."

"Why would we go there?"

Dewey sighed. He'd worked almost a double shift at the warehouse and didn't get that much sleep the night before. "Isn't that where the kid with the dreadlocks said we should meet him? That's what you said."

"No, no. The Grasso, not the Morgue. No way the Morgue."

"The *Grasso*?" Dewey was sure this was wrong. The Grasso Villa was an old headbanger hangout that catered to an aging stoner crowd. "Shannon, you definitely said the Morgue, man."

"No I didn't."

"Seriously, man, you did."

"No I didn't. I don't think."

"You don't think? So you're not sure."

"I'm pretty sure. Naw, I'm sure."

"You don't sound sure."

"I don't wanna drive all the way over there."

"But that's where they are," said Dewey. *Christ, he doesn't want to drive there.*

"No it isn't. You misunderstood."

"Man, you did say the Morgue. I mean, why would those trendy ass little weasels want to go to the Grasso? To see fucking Beerflesh?" The kids who wanted to buy the dope, by Dewey's judgment, were art student types dressed in fashionable rebellious-youth gear.

"They don't play there every night."

"Just about. They're sort of the house band, aren't they?"

"I dunno. All I know is that's what he said, the Grasso."

Dewey knew it was no use arguing with him, so why bother. They rode on in silence for a minute. Shannon broke it.

"Seriously, I wouldn't do this shit again myself, but, whatever. I wouldn't even be selling it if construction wasn't so fucked around here."

"I wouldn't do it again, looking at what happened to Todd." *Hey, Shannon brought it up.*

"Christ, man. That wasn't 'cause of the stuff or anything. He's all hung up about Clare," said Shannon. "He needs to get back to having a life, instead of just being a wino and watching porn movies all day."

"Yeah," said Dewey. Like cooking up some weird street drug Hobie Lautenschlager hunted up so Shannon could make a few bucks. They'd talked about it too many times, and Dewey didn't really want to argue. He decided to change the subject. "So are we gonna go see any movies at the thing, the marathon?"

"Is there anything that sounds good?" Shannon sounded unenthused.

Dewey pulled a leaflet from his coat pocket. "I'm kind of interested in this *Highway of Lost Souls*, which is tomorrow at eleven." He read aloud. "'The zombie apocalypse takes to the road! A lone teenage runaway hitchhiker finds that thumbing a ride has become even more dangerous than usual when—'"

"I heard about that one. It sounds stupid."

"Why?"

"Because it's supposed to all be about zombies driving around in cars. How is that different from just regular people in cars?"

"Okay. Let's see what else they got. Saturday at 9:30, *Peter, Peter, Child of Woe*, 1973. 'Peter Wilbury is mistakenly released from an

15

insane asylum fifteen years after stabbing to death his mother and his sadistic junior-high gym teacher when he caught them together in fla-grante—'"

"I don't mean in the morning. I don't want to go until afternoon at least."

"Saturday at one p.m., *Cannibal Camp 2: Eat it Raw*, 1996. 'Return to Camp Dahmer, where—'"

"Is that one of Hobie's Bongoville movies?"

"Yeah. I saw the first one."

"Fabulous? A laugh riot?"

"It wasn't terrible. I don't think you'd like it, though. The usual cute shit."

"They all are. I can't deal with Bongoville." Dewey didn't much like that studio's movies either, self-parodying campy schlock movies, though some were better than others. It was true that Hobie couldn't get enough of them, though otherwise he considered himself a so-phisticated film enthusiast.

"Well, then at 3:20, *Lovely Lepers, or the Devil's Harem*."

"That's more of that zany shit."

"No, actually, it's an Italian movie from 1958. I saw an article about it somewhere. Not a comedy. S'posed to be real creepy. 'On a remote Pacific island, three shipwrecked sailors encounter a bevy of entrancingly beautiful native girls . . .'"

"Subtitles?"

"I'm sure Hobie would want those if they're available, that kind of movie."

"If I wanna read, I'll get a book."

Dewey laughed, sort of. "Oh, c'mon."

"What about late afternoon, or is that just more Hobie bullshit? Aren't there any gay buttfucking movies? It's Hobie's marathon, after all."

"I dunno, man, fuck it." Dewey tossed the flyer over his shoulder into the back seat. Shannon had a big grudge against Hobie these days because of Todd and Hobie and the video store and all. Plus, Roni's job at the movie theater.

"I mean," said Shannon, "I don't know how Roni stands it, work-ing for that fat cocksucker. He gets to be more of a faggot all the time, too. Flapping his wrists and shit. She knew he'd try to make her work even later if she'd hung around tonight, that's why she wanted to meet at the Limbo."

16

"Yeah." Earlier, Shannon said it had been his idea to meet her there, but Dewey wasn't going to mention that. The silence resumed and stretched on as they continued up I-71 to the Grasso, where Dewey was certain their customers would not be found.

3
JAIME SPECULATES

Jaime had followed Roni all the way home from a distance of about a block and a half. She'd walked stiffly and never looked back over her shoulder. He didn't think she'd noticed him. She got to her house, went inside and turned on the lights. He was tempted to sneak up and peek in the windows to see what was happening. If Shannon was there, it probably meant they were going to fight. If not, Jaime wondered if she would cry once she realized she was alone. He liked to keep a lookout on things but decided not to risk it.

Once when keeping a lookout, a couple years before, Jaime had been peeking in the bathroom window at Shannon's house and saw Roni naked in the shower. Fortunately, he'd backed away before she saw him, otherwise Shannon would have been after him about that, wanting to kick his ass, which he'd sort of done a couple of times, wailed on him anyway. Still, he'd been kind of especially interested in her since then. She might not look as good now because she'd gotten a little chubbier, though not too bad really, not like Heather, even, and Heather looked okay, he thought, though other people said she looked like Miss Piggy from that kiddie show on TV. Jaime had never even been around a live naked girl before that time he saw Roni, except for his older sister, Cheryl Sue, who was great big and real unsightly that way, and his little sister, Dawnie, though she'd been too young to have breasts and stuff.

The only other girl he'd ever seen naked was the one he found in the woods, and she was dead at the time. She was also the only one he'd gotten to do any sex stuff with, which might not even count since she was dead and all. Cold and stiff, but she was still a girl. Kind of cute, too, even though she was Chinese and had that weird red hair, which Chinese people weren't supposed to have, he was pretty sure. They all had black hair on TV. Jaime didn't like to think about the way it ended up, after only a few days. She had gotten all bloated up so he was afraid she might burst open somewhere if he lay on her anymore, and she'd started to smell garbagey, even though it was real cold out then. He was sorry when she got that way, wept when he had to bury her. He wasn't sure he'd done a good job of that, either, since he wasn't able to dig a really deep hole, and had never gone back to look at her makeshift grave.

That was another reason why he was keeping an eye on Todd and Shannon. They'd been out there fucking that girl in the woods, and she died. So maybe they'd killed her, though it didn't look that way to him. Todd was the last one with her, and he was all upset when she started getting sick, ran away calling for Shannon and Dewey to come and help. She was dead a minute later, though. Jaime just wasn't sure what had happened, and he couldn't tell anybody about it because of what he'd done with her after he'd dragged her away.

He didn't feel like going home yet. The toilet was stopped up and the place was getting kind of stinky, and he wasn't sure how to fix it. It worried him because the stink might make somebody come upstairs and they'd find he was staying there in the attic apartment of the theater, which thus far nobody had bothered him about. In fact, nobody seemed to even know it was there, though it had an old mattress on the floor and even a working toilet, though it was real grungy inside and didn't fill up with water very well. But now the toilet was the big problem.

Thinking about toilets made him aware of his slight discomfort. He'd needed to take a piss back at the Limbo but didn't because he had to follow Roni. Well, might as well go back to the Limbo then, before it closed. At least the toilet there worked. Besides, he wanted

19

to know whether Shannon and Dewey had showed up back there. What with those kids that had come in, Jaime kind of suspected Shannon might be selling dope or something.

4

TODD AT HOME

Todd was in bed, sleeping fitfully, when a sense of impending doom began to kick in. It was like the room was filling up rapidly with water, was suddenly already filled, not with fresh or tap water but with thick, slimy, translucent green glop, like in a neglected aquarium. He took a deep breath, fearing he'd drown, or perhaps puke his guts out and then drown, but found he could breathe fitfully, as if uneven streams of air roped through the slime. The ceiling light was on above him and, though he'd never noticed it before, there was a stairway just beyond the door near the foot of his bed. A swarm of slithery creatures crawled in every direction beyond the door's threshold. Fearing they'd soon move forward into his room, get into his bed and squirm all over him, biting, scratching and oozing poisons, he closed his eyes in a hard squint, until he heard the thumping footsteps of something much larger and still more dreadful coming.

Blinking open and looking up, he saw Lenore, naked and hugely swollen like a saturated sponge, looming over the bed. Her red hair was mostly gone, and her slanted eyes seemed like empty sockets. Dark blood overflowed from her mouth, streaming down her body and across the floor in rivulets.

The room was now empty except for humid air, but the walls were soaked, buckling and reeking of mildew. He got out of bed, naked himself, and pushed at Lenore's bobbing balloon-like breasts. Rotten bilge poured out of her like a waterfall, submerging and drowning Todd.

He woke up, or thought he did. He lay flat on his back in a dry bed, but someone nearby, in bed beside him, was laughing. Gazing aside, he saw it was Clare. When did she come back, was she here all along and her absence had been a dream? She was in that old flimsy nightgown of hers from years ago, looking young and fresh as she did when he first knew her, but her eyes were all pupils and darting around, and her mouth was curved like the mask that represented comedy. Her laughter was mechanical, repetitive, coming from a windup device inside her. "Clare, what are you . . ." He tried to sit up but something heavy held him down, something around his neck. She laughed harder, tossing her head with merriment, eyes slit and entirely black, possessed.

"Clare, what is this thing on me? I can't get up!"

She leaned down, her grinning deathmask face nearly pressed against his, and spoke in a low, mocking voice. "*It's a little corpse.*"

He heard a scream and really woke up. He was in his rocking chair, near the TV. Clare was gone, there was no one. He must have screamed himself. The videocassette he'd been watching had run out, the VCR had shut off and the TV buzzed loudly.

Jesus, what the fuck brought that on? Wine, too much wine in one day. Wine and nothing to eat. He was seldom hungry anymore.

Shaken, he lifted the big open bottle of cheap-ass Rhine wine beside his chair on the floor and took a couple gulps. It was warm, and he choked a little getting it down. Rhino wine, that's what Clare used to say, back in the days when she'd drink with him, back when she had a sense of humor, before she got all caught up in UFOs and fallen angels and Jesus and all that crazy shit. He'd stopped drinking wine and switched to beer for a while, for pretty much the first year after she'd left, because of sad associations. But he didn't drink beer anymore, had switched back because wine didn't give him that pain he'd get under his right rib cage as bad as beer did. Plus, he didn't want to get a beer-belly again. Despite having no social life and no desire for one, he kind of liked the fact he was getting skinny like he'd been way back, though he also wondered if that meant he had cirrhosis of the liver or something. He never went out except to get more wine and cigarettes, and food, though mostly just microwave dinners. He dutifully ate one, or part of one, every day or so.

He yawned hard and long, almost hurting his jaw at its hinges, and snapped his mouth closed. He wondered what movie he'd been watching. He pressed the eject button on the VCR, and what came out was *Tight Teen Twats 17*. Okay, he remembered, he'd been watching that one again. It had some good scenes with one of his favorite girls in them, the young skinny one with long fluffy bottle-blonde hair growing out dark at the roots, and big mascaraed eyes, and who always whimpered, "Hrnt, Hrnt!" while she was getting fucked. She might have been saying, "hurts," but you couldn't tell. It couldn't have been hurting too much because when the scenes ended, usually with a facial, she'd always have a big toothy smile. She looked about twenty years old, in a video from probably twenty years before. In the scant dialogue included, he'd noticed she couldn't pronounce "r"s very well.

He had no idea who she was, there were always so many actresses' names scrolling fast down the screen at the start, especially with the anthologies. That was what most of the porn videos they'd carried at the shop were, and he'd taken most of them when it closed. Hobie didn't want them because he'd gone gay. Though he didn't take the gay ones either, they got tossed out.

He pushed the cassette back in. When he did, it sputtered and made a brief grinding sound, then quit with a slam. It was stuck. "Shit," he said. He hit eject again and, at that, it crunched loudly. "Aw, fuck." It occurred to him this video had at least a couple of his favorite "Hrnt, Hrnt," scenes on it.

He picked up the VCR and turned it upside down, shook it. No dice.

Reluctantly, he got up and stepped into the kitchen to get something to try and pry the cassette out with. He reminded himself to be careful, didn't want to fuck up the VCR. Though it might actually be better to save the tape and ruin that, since he could get another machine, though he'd have to go to the fucking mall tomorrow to get one, and in the meantime, a few hours at least, wouldn't be able to watch anything. Never find that tape again, though.

The kitchen, as usual, was a ghastly mess. He really should

straighten it up one of these days.

He looked in the silverware drawer, found an old butcher knife. It was about the only thing left in the drawer besides butter knives because all the other utensils were in the sink, along with almost all the dishes, though he seldom used them anymore. A screwdriver might have been better, but he didn't know where one was. He really needed to do the dishes. The sink was full of pretty foul stuff, including those frying pans he'd used earlier to cook up some of that worm shit for Shannon. He ran hot water into it, squirted some dish soap in, and let it fill up. That cut the smell some. Maybe he'd come back and do the dishes later if he felt up to it.

Back in the living room, he went to work on the VCR, trying to get the blade into the doored slot where the tape went in. It wouldn't go in very far. He might have to take that damn little door off. Before he tried to do that, he remembered to unplug the thing. He yanked the cord, and it whipped out of the wall socket. Settling back into his chair to look at it more closely, he considered how to deal with it. Should he push the knife in at the narrow side of the slot? No, it wouldn't fit. How about sideways across the top? Maybe there's a tab there holding the tape in . . .

Frustrated, he pushed the knife in hard, and the tape shifted. He turned the VCR upside down, kept fishing with the knife until it jarred forward and bit into his hand, between the thumb and forefinger. It stung, and blood welled out. *Fuck!*

He threw the knife down and looked at his hand. It bled pretty badly. Aggravated, he set the machine down hard onto the floor and, somehow, that made the machine disgorge the tape, sending it skidding across the floor and under the sofa.

Christ! Well, he had to deal with his cut hand before he did anything else. He went into the bathroom to look for some Band-Aids.

Crumpled on the bathroom floor were the pants he'd been wearing yesterday, and for the last few days. He'd forgotten he'd left them there and now wore only a t-shirt. There was, he recalled, shit in the pants. As happened every once in a while these days, he'd thought he'd just had to pass some gas but what came out was a big dollop of turd, so he'd had to wriggle quickly out of the pants. He didn't wear underwear very often, unless his balls were sore. There was a bunch of laundry to be done anyway, but he might want to wash the shit out of the pants in the bathtub first rather than contaminate his other clothes by just throwing them in the washer. Of course, that would slime up the bathtub as well. Life was just one damn chore after another.

He left the pants on the floor for the time being.

First, he needed a Band-Aid, and maybe some mercurochrome, if there was any. The cabinet in the bathroom was all full of expired bottles of Tylenol and tubes of backrub and jock itch ointment and stuff. No mercurochrome, but there was a bottle of hydrogen peroxide in the cabinet with a little bit left in it. Rummaging through, he found a couple of Band-Aid boxes, one empty and the other with a few spot Band-Aids that wouldn't be big enough at all. The cut still bled a little, blood streaking down his palm, so he went to the sink and held it under the cold water tap to stanch it. The blood reminded him of his dream, but he put it from his mind.

After a minute or so, it wasn't bleeding too much. He poured some of the peroxide over the cut, which stung a little. Maybe he'd get some more Band-Aids at the supermarket when he went there to get more bottles of wine, after it got light out.

Well, he wouldn't be able to do the dishes now, even if he'd wanted to.

Back in the living room again, he got down on the floor and looked under the sofa for the skidded-away tape. Damn, it was hard to get down on the floor, made his back really hurt. He didn't move that way often. Reaching under, he was mildly surprised to find something else, a little paperback book, looked like science fiction at a glance. He used to have a ton of those, mostly SF, but had gotten rid of most of them after Clare left. He just didn't want a whole lot of clutter around. He still had enough with all the VHS tapes. He told himself he'd lost interest in it all, turned off partly by Clare's UFO craziness, not that that had a lot to do with real science fiction. He'd still find books around sometimes, in closets and so forth.

He put the book in his injured right hand and reached in farther with his left, finding something else: the cassette. He put that on top of the book and, with his other hand pressed onto his aching back, took both and sat down in his rocker with a weary huff.

The videotape was definitely fucked up, lengths of brownish-gray tape sticking out of the back of it, crumpled. No use even trying to put it back in the VCR. Oh yeah, now he needed to see how bad the VCR was. So stupid of him to bang it on the floor. It might be totally croaked.

Lifting it from the floor, he set the VCR on the TV stand again.

He bent down, his back straining, and plugged the cords into the back of the TV set. Another tape sat on top of the TV, *Latex Dreamdolls*, a kind of arty porn movie in which inflatable sex dolls turned into real girls. He didn't feel like watching it again but, since it was handy, put it in.

The screen brightened, and on it, a rubbery red mouth disgorged white slime. Hey, it still played. He was surprised, his luck being so bad all the time. *Great, things are looking up*, he thought sarcastically as the scene switched to a large black dildo jabbing in and out of a smooth and taut behind.

He looked at the book. The cover showed a sinister looking, bulb-headed alien with huge black eyes wielding a bloodied machete under the title: *Plan 666: Sex, Satanism and Ritual Slayings in the UFO-Crazed Cults of Armageddon.*

Well, what the fuck, it was one of Clare's UFO books, though this one he didn't remember. Great. Surprised she didn't take it with her. She had a bunch of books on the subject and they were all gone on the day he'd come home and found she'd vamoosed. She must have misplaced this one. Clare hadn't been much tidier than he was, especially after she went through her big sea-change.

He hadn't read a book in a long time and, opening this one at a random page, found he had a little trouble focusing on the text. He'd wondered lately whether he was losing his sight. He'd been seeing a lot of floaters, and they could be really distracting. They ranged from swirling brownish blotches resembling coffee stains to odd, sketchy black figures that looked like some kind of evil bugs. He even wondered whether the trouble he had sometimes while watching movies, of colors getting more and more strange and figures distorted, came from a vision problem rather than the TV itself. Though it was an old TV, and it mostly only happened when he watched porn videos. But then, that was pretty much all he watched, anymore. Maybe you could literally go blind from drinking. If his eyes were too fucked up for him to read books anymore, he wasn't sure he wanted to know. Oh well, maybe he'd try to read it, maybe not.

But he kept leafing through the book, barely noticing the frisky girls half-undressed in black rubber slutgear on his TV screen. He came across a passage about that Paradise Threshold group Clare used to talk endlessly about.

Well within the long tradition of American apocalypticism, and like the Kindred cult which had preceded it, Paradise Threshold originated with the testimony of Delbert Wingdale, who claimed to have been abducted and held captive for eleven years by the Niff, bodiless alien spirits stranded upon the Earth for millennia, whose habitat is a system of catacombs deep inside the Earth . . .

5

SHANNON AND DEWEY AT THE GRASSO

Shannon and Dewey pulled into the parking lot at the Grasso Villa. The lot was about half full, though it was near closing time. The damaged marquee over the entrance said, in letters of varying design:

FRI BEARFLESH

SAT QUEENSRYCHE TRIBUTE

Dewey was somewhat satisfied to see he'd been right about Bearflesh, but wasn't going to point it out. The music coming from inside was muffled and distorted.

Hunching against the night air, they stepped fast through the front entrance. The fat, greasy kid with the razored mullet at the ticket window didn't bother asking for their IDs, just took the cash they held out and banged the ink stamper over the backs of their hands while talking animatedly over his shoulder to a petite girl with a white-blonde perm and heavy make-up on her face that failed to cover up her acne. She looked about fifteen and was smoking a cigarette without inhaling. She nodded but kept looking away from the fat kid as he spoke, apparently not wishing to allow him to think she was much engaged. *Good luck, chump*, thought Dewey.

The music boosted hugely in volume as they pulled the heavy, green-lacquered interior door open and stepped inside to merge with the murmur of talk and the stench of beer and piss. The hall appeared vast because of the sparseness of the crowd, mostly the usual young-ish-but-aging clientele with a few fresh-faced teenagers scattered among them, under lights that seemed bright above but provided lit-tle illumination below. Tables were bunched together in the middle of the place, leaving about thirty feet of space in front of them for dancing. Nobody was on stage, but a drum set was there, along with a couple worn-looking guitars on stands. The bass drum had a logo on it, BEARFLESH, along with a crude drawing of a growling griz-zly's head. A record was playing at high volume, 'Practice What You Preach' by Testament.

The crowd milled around or sat at tables drinking and talking, leaning their heads close to hear each other over the racket. Dewey sat at an empty table. Shannon leaned on a chair.

"Okay," said Shannon, "so you were right about Beerflesh. Con-gratulations."

"Told ya," said Dewey. "Where are the kids?"

"Don't worry, they're around here somewhere. This is where they said, man, I'm sure."

"Maybe they were kidding."

"No, they said here. Maybe they've come to appreciate classic headbanger culture."

"Yeah, I'm sure that's the case."

"They're probably here for the pussy, really," said Shannon. "I told them about the Mean Stevies phenomenon, and they were in-trigued." "The Mean Stevies" was Shannon's term for some of the girls who hung out at the Grasso, or used to. It was an old quip of his, from ten or fifteen years ago. Back then, a lot of girls you'd see at the place seemingly tried to achieve a resemblance to Stevie Nicks, cultivating the singer's spazzy ringlets, flouncy dresses and lipsticked pout. But instead of appearing soft and feminine, Grasso girls tended to still look harsh, as people on the grungy west side of Stankerton generally tended to be. Looking around, Dewey did see a few females of more or less the Stevie description, but those few were looking a bit haggard, maybe because it was late.

Anyway, saying that to those kids would make them think you

were a pitiful oldster. Hopefully Shannon hadn't done so.

"Man, place could use some more lights," said Shannon, digging into his shirt pocket for a cigarette. "Same old shit. Could be the Beers are doing one more set, or not."

"I hope not." Dewey didn't really want to hear Bearflesh, though he hoped they'd missed the Queensryche tribute band.

The stage lit up and the members of Bearflesh came out and lifted guitars from their stands, flamboyantly dressed but paunchy, most of them, with hair at least shoulder-length but starting farther back on their foreheads than it used to. The singer, Billy D'Amato, came out in red spandex pants and boots, a wifebeater t-shirt, a considerable belly hanging out of it and over the front of his pants. However, his frizzled black elbow-length hair looked the same as it had for decades. *Maybe,* Dewey thought, *that meant it was a wig. Had it always been a wig?*

An old tired-looking guy with a grizzled beard and military hat went up to the mike, his voice full of radio-announcer enthusiasm. "Ladies and gentleman! Once again, the famous Grasso Villa brings you Stankerton favorites, *Bearflesh!*"

Some in the crowd yammered weakly in response, and there was even a little applause. "*Beeeeeer-fleeeeesh!*" someone bellowed drunkenly. Obviously, they'd already played and this was the last bit for the evening.

"Awright, Stankerton!" Billy yelled in a fake gravelly voice. "It's gettin' late, but rock and roll never cums, or what the fuck, I dunno. What day is it, Saturday already? What are people still doing here, losers? Go the fuck home."

"Friday," someone called out. "Saturday morning," said another.

"Okay, it don't matter, 'cause you know what?" He amped up his voice. "You know what, Stankerton? We gonna open up a can o' kickass here t'night! That's right!" He grabbed at his crotch and yanked upward, possibly as a rude gesture, or just to loosen the spandex a bit.

"Awright then! This here is a song we did earlier, we got a request for a reprise. It's about bitches that want to wrap you around their little finger, you know? Sure you do. But what I do is, I wrap 'em around my fuckin' dick! It's called 'Swallow My Love,' one two three—"

Feedback shrieked, drums were pounded and power chords struck as the familiar mock-frenzied ritual ensued. This had been a standard number of theirs for years, having once been featured on a local radio station.

"Well, that's awesome," said Shannon, leaning close and speaking into Dewey's ear to be heard over the roaring music. "I'm gonna look around for the weasels."

"They're closing in like a half hour or less," said Dewey.

"Awright, awright." Shannon walked off.

Sitting by himself, enduring the music, Dewey fretted. Just being here kind of depressed him. He and Shannon used to hang at Grasso's a lot when they were in high school, and maybe for a few years after, but only once in a while in the last couple years, especially since Shannon had gotten married. Though in fact, Dewey hardly went out anymore unless he was with Shannon. He especially didn't like seeing people there he used to see around, especially not people he used to know, and he didn't much like that screaming speedfreak metal they played these days, especially when they sang in monster voices or tried to add rap shit to it.

Besides, the last time they'd been there, Shannon had been real drunk and got so he was fucking with people—strangers—which he did sometimes, a certain level of drink bringing out the sociopath in him, and they'd gotten thrown out by security. But that was like six months ago or maybe longer.

Just the same, Dewey was more worried than ever before about what Shannon was getting into—or maybe, more worried than he'd been since the first year after high school when he really seemed to go kamikaze for a while. This wasn't as bad as that, but the fucker was getting pretty reckless again. Dewey thought it was mostly because of work. Construction was down, and he hadn't been getting a lot of painting jobs since, well, last winter really. That was probably the real cause of the strife at home with Roni, too. Dewey hoped so, anyway. He liked Roni, even though she pretty much ignored him. Of course, he himself hadn't had a real girlfriend in so long now it was embarrassing. He even sometimes told Shannon he was in touch with his old girlfriend Alta, when he really hadn't heard from her in well over a year.

Then there was that incident with a kind of cute girl hitchhiker who turned out to be a guy. Oh well, fuck that, he'd just been drunk.

He ambled over to the bar, some distance from the stage and off in an alcove, to get a beer. He stood against a wall, still farther back, drinking and wincing as he watched the band. Fucking Bearflesh, still at it. At this point, the only members he could identify were Billy and the lead guitarist, Ed "Buzzy" Napper, the leader and only original member. White-bearded and very saggy, in a headband and shades, he looked like he was about seventy, though he must have been more like fifty. Billy had been in the band nearly as long. He used to be skinny and popular with girls. Oh, well, that's life. Now they were doing an old song of theirs titled "Kill the Pain" or something like that, another one they'd been doing forever, though it sounded like they wrote it in five minutes.

Dewey didn't watch the band for long, finishing his beer up fast and going for another one. When he returned to his spot by the wall he was looking around at the girls. As he went on drinking, his self-consciousness faded and he looked at them more brazenly. After a few drinks he didn't care what they thought, though he'd still be careful about staring at a chick who was with a guy. He wasn't trying to pick anybody up or anything, hadn't even thought about really trying to do that for years.

After a while, Dewey started wondering a little about where Shannon had gone off to. Wasn't going to find those kids, he figured. They were probably at the Morgue all along.

He finally spotted Shannon, sitting with some people at a table to the back. At first he thought it might be those guys he was supposed to sell to after all, but no, it was that one guy he knew who used to work at the garage out by, whatshisname, Chet's place. He was with some real homely chick. Dewey didn't feel like going over. Shannon was different, knew too many people, he was always running into somebody and standing around shooting the shit for a half hour.

Bearflesh broke into a ragged cover of Blue Oyster Cult's "7 Screaming Diz-Busters" that they'd also been doing forever.

He kept glancing back at this one girl who was standing by herself and was really cute, a knockout, a tall, slender, long-haired blonde in a form-fitting dress. Great ass in it, too. Maybe that was a fashion, punk or whatever, he didn't even know anymore. She was way too young for him. Wouldn't have paid any attention to him even if he was her age. He made himself turn his head away. Useless.

But he soon looked back. She was tossing her hair, smoking, pre-occupied. Her lipstick, he saw, was an odd shade of pink. It looked good on her. She was sweet. On impulse, Dewey wandered over nearer to her. Not that he was going to try to talk to her or anything.

When he got over there, within about six feet of her, the chick looked up and back at him, hard. She must have noticed him watching her. She didn't look pissed off, just defiant. He looked away for a few moments, and when he glanced back, she was smiling off in another direction. A young, skinny guy with a multicolored mohawk, wide and stiff as a peacock's tail, and wearing a Sex Pistols t-shirt, sat down beside her. She threw her arms around his neck and cuddled. *Lucky fucker.*

Dewey moved off, annoyed at himself. He wasn't ever going to try and talk to her anyway, so what was that about? He needed to take a piss, then get Shannon and get out of there. No weasels, he was sure.

The men's room was crowded and noisy. The brew of community urine was intense and a little sickening from five or six feet outside it. On the way there, down a short corridor, young guys who were exiting passed Dewey, laughing and stomping along. They all seemed so much like kids to him. Get them in a big bunch and they're all excited, trying to impress each other and shit, just like back on the playground. Not that long ago for them.

As Dewey took the door handle, somebody came up from behind and grabbed his arm. "Hey, man," came a loud voice, "you checkin' out my bitch?"

He whirled around. It was Shannon, smirking.

"Man, don't fuckin' do that. About to take a piss." They stepped into the restroom. It was more crowded than the rest of the club.

"How'd you like that guy's Don Eagle, wasn't that delightful?"

"That was a mohawk," said Dewey, "not a Don Eagle. A Don Eagle is short."

"I stand corrected. I think what I'll do is, I'll run down to the Hair Happening Salon tomorrow and get me one like it. The babes will get wet at the sight of me."

Dewey snorted a sort-of laugh. "Not me, I don't have enough hair left." He went up to the urinal and started pissing.

"That's your excuse for everything," said Shannon. "Anyway, see, I told you the young folk were hangin' here."

"Yeah, that kid with the mohawk could get his ass kicked out in the parking lot here, too. For trespassing in headbanger land." Done, he wagged his dick. "What about the weasels?"

"I can't find them. They must have split. Anyway, I bet I could— Whoa! What the fuck?!"

Dewey turned his head, saw what Shannon had seen: a girl with long red hair, not orange-red but really fire-engine red hair, petite and foxy, in a black leather jacket over a frilly white mini-dress, black-and-white striped hose, and tan clodhopper shoes, was half-strutting and half-staggering across the restroom. She went into one of the doorless toilet stalls. She yanked the hose down past her knees, pulled up her little dress, no panties and, damn, no pubic hair, and sat. She tossed her wild red locks and looked at nothing, seemingly oblivious to nearly all the eyes in the place turning her way. A burbling came from under her.

Dewey felt a wave of dread pass through him. That hair. The girl in the woods had really red hair too, just like that. Well, pretty close. She had been Asian and this one was white, but the hair . . .

"All right, baby!" someone called. There was much hooting and laughter, while a couple guys shook their heads and a very few others ignored the spectacle completely. She, in turn, seemed faraway, perhaps lost in thought.

Shannon strode over and stood right in front of her, folding his arms. "Say, I'm not complaining, but I think you're in the wrong room, honey," he said.

The girl seemed to wake a bit, smiled up at him, but didn't laugh. "The other room was crowded."

"That would be the ladies' room," said Shannon.

She shrugged, still smiling, though a bit vaguely. Dewey had finished up and turned around, a bit embarrassed to watch her openly, but everybody else was, so he did too. She was still peeing. Shannon stood there staring and smiling, brazen even for him. She wiggled a bit and reached for the roll of toilet paper.

"Whoa, you had to pee a lot," he said.

"I know," said the girl. She tore off some paper, wiped, and pulled her hose up. "Thank you, gentlemen," she said, not sounding sarcastic at all, and stepped around Shannon, weaving a bit as she went. Obviously stoned, no surprise there. She'd have to be stoned or nuts, or a total slut. Or all three.

"Jesus," said Dewey to Shannon. "Well, anyway, those guys aren't here and they're gonna close—"

"Hold it, man, I'm going to get this chick before somebody else does," said Shannon, elbowing past him, after her.

"C'mon, she's probably with somebody," said Dewey. "Besides, we don't really have time, man." But Shannon was already out of the room.

Christ, thought Dewey, hurrying after him. Last time he picked somebody up it didn't go so well. Doesn't he even remember? That whole thing in the woods, and Todd and all? With bright red hair, even?

Dewey saw that the redhead chick was already walking across the far side of the club. The band was done, there was no music at all, and a lot of people had left, it looked like. They must be closing, about to announce. Shannon came up behind her, put his hand on her back. She turned, looked up. They were too far away for Dewey to hear, and too many other people milled around for him to even see very clearly. He thought maybe she wouldn't like Shannon doing that, might even turn around and slap him or something, but instead, wow, she twirled around like a dancer and pushed her face close to his. He grabbed her upper arms, seemed to be holding her up.

A boyfriend might come up any minute, or some other girls that she's with. Be nice if there was just one other girl, one about like her. *Yeah, right.*

She laced an arm around Shannon's neck, looked like she was urging him to dance, though the music was off. He did a couple comic steps, stopped, and at that she let go, waving her arms around and swaying. Maybe swaying a little too much. She tripped and fell backwards against some guy behind her. Shannon caught her and pulled her to him. She threw her arms around him as if she could barely control them, and put her head on his shoulder, like he was her hero, or maybe like she was too exhausted to stand up anymore by herself. Either way, it looked pretty phony to Dewey, like she was putting on a show. You had to watch out for girls like that.

Shannon helped her over to a table that had just been vacated by a couple who were up dancing, though a purse and some drinks were still left on it. Dewey stepped over and sat down with them. The chick put her head down, once again a bit flamboyantly, but after a moment rose up and grabbed the purse. She opened it, rifled inside, took out a pack of cigarettes. *Uh-oh, that was somebody else's purse, wasn't it?* Unless she was there with those people who'd gotten up from the table.

Shannon, fixated on the chick, didn't even notice Dewey sitting there. "So," said Dewey, "did you give up on finding those guys?"

"Oh, hey, I almost forgot about you, dude." He tapped the girl on the shoulder. "Hey, this here's my main man, Dewey."

She was beautiful close up, delicate features like a small child, heavy eyelashes but no apparent makeup, dazzling green eyes. She looked at Dewey, smiled as if childishly delighted at the sight of him,

raised a hand delicately and twirled her fingers for a moment. "Hi."
Dewey had seen this sort of greeting before, usually from stoner
chicks who knew they were cute. Even so, he smiled and nodded a
little.

But he leaned over close to Shannon to whisper to him. "C'mon,
man, she must be with somebody."

"Well, I dunno. Hey, girl. You here by yourself?" he asked her,
raising his voice to be heard over the music.

"Hmm?" She tossed her hair, looked around. Stunning. Could be
a model, a movie star, even.

"You here with anybody? Where are your friends?"

"Friends? Oh, Okay. Let's see. They, ummm . . . they were here,
but . . . oh wait, I'm confused. That was, like, the other day." She was
murmuring and hard to hear, and Shannon kept leaning closer and
putting his hand to his ear. She laughed, making eye contact first with
Shannon, then, only briefly, with Dewey, then back to Shannon.

Story of my life, thought Dewey.

"How'd you get here?"

"I think somebody dropped me off." She gazed around again.

"Are you looking for somebody?"

"No." She put her unlit cigarette in the ashtray, leaned her head
on top of her folded arms on the table.

"You okay and everything?"

"I'm tired." She grabbed the purse in front of her, dug through it,
pulled out the pack of cigarettes again. "Merit menthol," she said.
"Yuck!"

"Aren't those your cigarettes?"

"It's not mine," she said, shoving the purse away. She glanced
mischievously at Shannon. "Have you got any cigarettes that aren't
menthol?"

"Uh, sure." He pulled out a pack of filterless Camels, shook it
expertly to make some shoot up from the opening.

She laughed. "Yikes! That's okay." She grabbed the Merit from
the ashtray, put it in her mouth, dug through the purse some more.
"There's got to be a lighter in here."

"Here," Shannon said, offering a Bic lighter. She leaned forward
to light up. Big pupils in those strange eyes. She was really stoned.
Shannon lit up a Camel.

"So what about those kids?" said Dewey. "You forget about them
too?"

"What kids?"

"The weasels."

"Oh yeah, them." His eyes were still on her. "They're not here, I guess."

"We better split then, huh? This place is about ready to close." The girl had her head down on the table now, and was looking at Shannon with the air of a tired toddler. "I suppose," said Dewey, tapping an ash off his cigarette.

Dewey leaned again toward Shannon, spoke into his ear. "Is she awright? Look at her eyes."

"Yeah, very nice. Hey, babydoll? You're beat, aren't you? Tired?"

"Mmmm," she said.

"We better go. What about Roni?"

"Who?" said Shannon, crinkling his face in puzzlement, like he'd never heard the name before.

"Your wife, Veronica."

"What about her?"

"We we're supposed to pick her up at the Limbo." *Plus,* thought Dewey, *she exists.*

"She's left there by now," said Shannon. He put his hand on the chick's shoulder. "Say girl, you wanna go somewhere else?"

"I just want to go to bed," she said, keeping her head down and eyes closed.

Dewey almost shook his head. *Wow. Talk about asking for it.*

He glanced over the girl again, thought of what he'd seen in the men's room. Well, on the other hand . . . Pass up an opportunity like this? Would he, if he picked her up hitchhiking? But, no.

"Hey, bud, this is our table," said a guy standing near, in a deep, threatening voice. Dewey looked up. An unshaven guy and a girl, the girl looked annoyed, the guy a little drunk. *Wants to impress the girlfriend, probably.* Not a big guy, but trying to act tough.

"Greg, don't," said the girl with him, scolding, a little worried. *That should help some.*

"I guess you left it, man. No reserved tables," said Shannon.

"Say again?" said the guy, glaring, trying to act bad.

"No reserved tables at the Grasso. You want to keep your table, you gotta stay at it."

"Like shit," said the guy.

"Greg, just get me my purse," said the girl. The guy, Greg, reached over and yanked the purse up by its strap, handed it over to the girl.

She opened it, looked through, frowned but said nothing. Greg folded his arms and scowled. He looked a little silly to Dewey, and probably more so to Shannon, who broke out laughing.

"Awright, Greg, the table's yours, my man. Enjoy." Shannon put his arm around the chick who had remained still through the exchange, not opening her eyes, even. But now she did, threw her head back, fingers through her hair, and stood up, putting her arm around Shannon's waist and her head on his shoulder. She was holding the other girl's pack of cigarettes in her hand, but if that girl noticed, she didn't say anything.

They stepped off together across the ballroom toward the exit, and Dewey followed after. Dewey thought he might have heard this Greg guy say something behind them, but nobody turned around.

They went out the door, stepped over to the T-Bird. As Shannon went around and unlocked the door, the chick was hunching her shoulders and wrapping her arms around herself. She had a jacket on, but it was cold out.

Shannon got in the car, reached over the back seat and opened the back door for her. Dewey opened the side door, got in. "Cold?" asked Shannon as she dropped into the back seat, shuddering.

"No," she said, "I'm fine now."

"It'll warm up in here in a minute," said Shannon. He started the engine.

"Okay if I lie down back here?" she asked.

"By all means, suit yourself." Dewey watched in the mirror as she snuggled down and pulled up her legs. For a moment, he could see up her dress: nice thighs in that black and white pantyhose. And nothing underneath it. Maybe something would happen, but it was up to Shannon.

6

RONI AT HOME

When Roni got home, she slammed the door, flopped down in an armchair in the living room, put her face in her hands for a minute, then tossed her head back with a scowl. She was not only furious at Shannon, but mad at herself for crying. Fuck him, she didn't care if he came home at all. Fucking dealing again, God knows what he's getting into now.

She didn't want to think about it any further, not tonight. Was there some of that fucking beer in the fridge? She stepped into the kitchen to check, and yes, there were four bottles of Mex Negri. She wasn't going to let herself drink them all; she didn't want to make herself sick and still be sick tomorrow at work, or to gain weight, or for Shannon to come lollygagging in and find her a little soused and the beer all gone. She could just hear him: "What, you drank all my fucking Negris? Sheesh!"

Shannon Boner, her husband. Couldn't believe she'd married a Boner. At least she hadn't taken his name. No way was she going to be Veronica Boner.

She fretted about work. Some church group was raising a stink about the posters for the marathon Hobie had come up with that said "Satan Is Lord" in blood-dripping lettering and showed a scene of a wild-eyed bare-breasted Asian girl with a gruesome, gore-dripping hole in her chest, holding out a blood-dripping heart to the viewer. This, Hobie had said, was from a movie titled *Succubus, the Girl of Prey*, that was supposed to be shown Sunday night. The church group objected to both the reference to Satan and the image of the girl and, in a letter to Hobie, shared with the local news media, made reference to the Westside Slasher, but hadn't directly mentioned the rumor the Slasher's victims' hearts had been cut out.

The slasher thing brought to mind that time a couple years before when a guy tried to drag her into his car outside the vintage clothing shop where she worked as she was waiting at the bus stop. He may have seen her there before and knew when she got off and would be at the stop. He was a thirtyish guy who looked very straight, balding with blond hair in a widow's peak. She didn't know cars, but it was a small black car. He had a big weird grin, showed a lot of gums and his teeth were dull yellow and had cracks in them. Looked like he was delighted as he pulled her forward in a strong grip, until she, in desperation, bit his hand until he yowled and let go.

She ran back to the shop where her boss, Helen, an older woman, was fortunately still present. The car charged up and sped away. She didn't get the license number. Helen thought she should call the police, but she didn't want to because she was frazzled and wanted to go home. Helen gave her a ride home. She hadn't worked there much longer.

The phone rang. Shannon? Should she even answer? Let him think she didn't make it home. It rang three times more. No, she'd better answer it, but if it was him, she'd hang up as soon as he started talking.

Picking up the phone, she said "Hello?" in a voice affected to sound bored.

"Umm, Veronica?" Not Shannon. "This is Benny."

Oh, for Christ's sake, this she needed about now. "Do you know what time it is?"

"I'm sorry to call, I was just about to give up. I was only going to let it ring seven times."

"It's about two in the morning."

"I didn't wake you up, did I? You got the phone right away." She groaned, and he spoke again quickly. "I'm sorry to bother you, but I have to talk to someone about Hobie. I'm very concerned about him. This isn't about me, okay?"

"I'm not sure I should be—"

"I think you already know what I'm talking about. Don't you? Unless you're in denial."

In denial. She considered hanging up.

"He's changed. He's like a different person. He's living in a solipsistic world of his own, indifferent to the rest of humanity."

Solipsistic? Hoo boy. Well, it was true Hobie had been acting distracted lately, but it seemed to her he did that every so often. In her presence, he talked in an odd way, as if expressing his thoughts not to her, but to himself.

"He's just that way, Benny," she said.

"No no no, no!" Benny's voice cracked. "It's not him. It's that drug he's on, it's transforming him."

"What drug?"

"You mean you actually don't know? He's on that worm drug."

"Worm?"

"Yes, worm, also known as Verum Deus by the Satanist cult that created it. The mind-shattering drug that causes acute disorientation and moral confusion. It's a very dangerous fad."

Moral confusion? "That doesn't sound like Hobie."

"I wouldn't have thought so either. He used to be the kind of person who had too much respect for his body to pollute it, but something drew him to this. I'm surprised he hasn't mentioned it to you. Are you sure he hasn't?"

"Yes, I'm sure he hasn't said anything about a drug."

"And he doesn't even seem any different to you?" This sounded like a contemptuous accusation.

"To be frank, I think Hobie might be behaving differently toward you for personal reasons."

"Just what are you implying?"

"Look, Benny, it's two in the morning, I worked all day and I have my own problems to deal with. Besides, I need to keep this phone clear. I'm expecting a call." A lie, though Shannon might call, or the cops might if he'd had a car accident.

Benny said, "I'm sorry if I sound angry. I'm dealing with a lot of anger right now because of things that have happened between Hobie and myself, of which I gather you're aware—"

"Really, I have to go now. I'll talk to you about this later, okay?"

"Will you really? Do you even care?"

"Yes, I'll talk to you later."

Benny sighed. "All right then," he said, all pissy, and with that, he hung up.

Good grief. She hung up the phone, grabbed the remote, turned on the TV. She punched the remote, ran through a number of channels showing stuff that looked really uninteresting. So many channels, so much shit. A logo appeared on the screen, *Trumpet His Word!* with the "t" in the form of a stylized cross, followed by "with your host . . ." *There we go, fucking Dr. Trumpeter Landfrey again. Is he ever not on?*

The phone rang again. *Jesus fuck!* It had better not be Benny calling back or she'd rip him a new asshole. He'd like that, probably. And if it was Shannon, she'd just hang up.

"Veronica, dear, you weren't sleeping, were you?" Great, it was Hobie. He and Benny were the only people who called her Veronica except for doctors and job interviewers and the like.

"No, no such luck."

"I'm just so up about the marathon. How do you think it's going?"

"It's a really good turnout. The attendees act like they're having fun." Not that she could say the same about herself.

"You know, honestly, the entire event is so much about my own desire to be a filmmaker, about the different directions I'm pulled in." *Uh oh, here we go again, the continuing story of Hobie and his dream to be a great auteur-type horror movie director.* ". . .on the one hand, I adore the raucous humor and iconoclastic spirit of the Bongoville fare, especially the films directed by Marty the Martian himself but, far more deeply than that I'm drawn to the dark aesthetic of Scalabrino and the other Italian '70s masters whose films really laid the groundwork for the extreme horror that's emerging today. Though none of the current generation, anywhere in the world, have come close to surpassing Scalabrino, in my view. That the two of them, Marty and Sab, worked together for a time has always fascinated me, though it's unsurprising that they finally became estranged."

Marty the Martian? Whatever. "You should write a book about it, Hobie," she said. In fact, he used to have a horror movie fanzine titled *Corpses Dreaming* or something like that. There had only been a couple issues, almost everything in them written by Hobie himself, and much of it about himself, so Shannon had said. She didn't care in any case. As Hobie knew, but here he was subjecting her to this boring shit at fucking two a.m.

"Oh, but what I really long to do is to make films, not to discuss them. I realize it so much now, that it's what I've always aimed for, almost unconsciously, because it seemed so out of my reach. To be the master of the spectacle. That is, I want to get to the real essence of film, of the horror cinema. The experience of it. The group aspect and the individual aspect. Widespread disaster and personal danger. But I've always been so misdirected. Always preparing to live, rather than being in the moment, you know? It's like what Kafka said, all his life had been a hesitation before birth. Well, no more!"

Yeah, right. She changed the subject. "Say, not to be a bummer but I should tell you, they showed one of the movies on your schedule on local TV tonight."

"Oh, I know! Did you see that?! It's the US release cut, butchered a second time for television. Truly a travesty and desecration of one of Scalabrino's greatest works. Fortunately, what we're showing is the director's version, not *Scream* but *7 Masks*."

"Director's cut, huh?"

"Oh, so much more than that!" He laughed. "It's a personal testament to the ages!"

Maybe Benny was right, he was acting pretty weird. "Are you okay, Hobie?"

"Okay, you ask?" He chortled for a long minute. It sounded almost like choking.

"You've been acting like you're awfully . . ." She considered what word to use. "Enthusiastic."

"I'm altogether delirious over the marathon! Wait 'til you see what special events I have planned!"

"Oh, say, I wanted to ask. Did you really mean to have the admission fee be the same on Saturday and Sunday as tonight? That's what the sign by the ticket booth says."

"Yes, I want to encourage people to go for the full experience of the schedule as I've arranged it." Okay, that hardly made sense, but it was his party. Though she'd be the one to have to argue with people about it.

"Another thing . . . that bunch of wacko Christians was still hanging around outside protesting your posters when I left tonight, and Channel 9 had a truck out there earlier, filming those hanged scarecrows you put up over the entrance."

"Are you serious? Fantastic! I couldn't be more thrilled!"

She thought about mentioning Benny's call, decided not to. "I'm glad you feel that way. But I really have to go now, okay?"

"Veronica, you've been an incredible help to me with the whole affair. I'm so grateful you came early and worked the ticket booth even, when Stella called in. Omigod, I almost forgot, this is another reason I'm calling! She's not coming in tomorrow either. I *hate hate hate* to ask, but could you do that again tomorrow, be in at about seven o'clock?"

She stifled a groan. Seven o'clock, that was about five hours away. Well, it would get her away from Shannon, if he even comes home. "Sure, but I really need to go to bed right now."

"You're an angel. We'll get through this, dear. It's only through Sunday, and then everything's over! Bye-bye now! Remember, Satan is Lord!" He chortled again and hung up.

Jesus. Obviously he was a lonely guy, but he had Benny who wanted to be with him, so why not bend *his* ear? Hobie acted real faggoty himself, but he seemed sometimes to be contemptuous of other gay men. He was all screwed up, really. Like everybody in this fucking town.

She went to the kitchen and got another bottle of Mex Negri. Maybe it would help her sleep. She was going to have to find out about this drug Benny mentioned. Maybe that was what was happening with Hobie. What did he call it, worm?

Hey, wait. What if that's what Shannon's dealing?

47

7

SHANNON, DEWEY AND THE GIRL

Shannon was driving, Dewey in the passenger seat and the gorgeous chick in the back, lying down. Redhead with green eyes, looks about twenty and totally foxy, and stoned out of her gourd. *Damn!* He felt like he'd hit the jackpot, but at this point in life, he just didn't know what to do with the prize.

He took a hit off a fresh joint out of the glove compartment and considered. Couldn't take her home, that was for certain. Not being sure he wanted to fuck her that badly, tonight anyway, was the weird thing. He didn't think it was because of being loyal to Roni. Why shouldn't he cheat on her? She'd been such a bitch lately. Besides, they didn't fuck very often anymore, not for the last six months or so. So why shouldn't he? Maybe he was reluctant because he'd been wanking off a couple-three times this week and wasn't totally sure he could fuck very well tonight if he tried. Making a bad impression was a drag, hadn't happened to him much that way, but he hated even a smidgen of that.

Gotta do something with her. She was way too good to just pass up and let go.

Dew, shit, he wasn't going to do anything but fret about her. He always was afraid of getting the clap ever since that one time fucking fifteen years ago. Or maybe that was an excuse, he was chicken, or whatever. Too bad, but that was how it was. Besides, he couldn't take her home either. He lived with his grandma and she'd freak.

When he glanced at the rear-view mirror, she was watching him calmly, not nervous at all, but like, waiting for him to do whatever it turned out he wanted to do. He kept watching her back, going back and forth between the road and the mirror. His kind of girl, used to be anyway, before he was married. Dewey was being quiet, sulking. Apparently, this situation coming up had put him in a snit. Really, he was getting to be as bad as Roni.

He handed the joint over to Dewey. "So, sweet thing, what's your name?" he called out.

"Hmm?"

"You got a name?"

"Sky," she seemed to say.

"What?"

"Sky," she said. "That's my name. Sky."

"Say again?"

"Sky. Like, you know, the sky. S-K-Y."

"Your name is Sky? Your real name?"

"Yes." She sounded a bit bored, like she'd had this conversation a few times before.

"Your parents must have been spaced-out hippies, right?" Dewey gave him a scolding look, but he just shrugged.

"No. Sort of."

"Well, my name's Shannon, and this, again, is my man, Dewey. I don't know if that's his real name or not." The car jounced some as he offered his right hand, backward. Her grip was very light, as so often with girls. He glanced over his shoulder, and she seemed to wink at him as though there was a fun secret between them. *Wow, did she really wink?* Maybe her face was just twitching or something because she was stoned.

She also reached out to shake hands with Dewey, her hand over his shoulder, though at first he didn't notice. "Shake hands, man," said Shannon.

As if waking suddenly, Dewey jolted up, turned, and, after hesitating, took her hand for the briefest moment. "Nice to meet you," he said. She smiled at him almost as intimately as she did at Shannon. *Chick likes everybody.* She fell back into the seat as if exhausted at the effort, stretched out, laid her sweet head down and closed her eyes. Dewey hit the joint again, hard, and handed it back to Shannon, coughing.

"So how'd you like that band back there, Sky?" said Shannon.

"Wha-aat?"

"The live band at the club back there, the old guys."

"They were okay," she said.

"You know what they're called?"

"No."

"Their name is supposed to be Bearflesh, like, a bear's flesh, a grizzly bear or whatever? But everybody calls them Beerflesh 'cause now they're fat from drinking beer. Pretty funny, huh?"

"Beerflesh?"

"Yeah, like, you know, beer makes you fat. It's also supposed to mean, like, bare flesh, like naked bodies. I mean, the original name, Bearflesh."

"Ha," she said. "Hey, can I have a hit?" Shannon shrugged, a bit annoyed that she didn't really laugh, passed the joint over his shoulder to her.

"Awright, thanks." She took a long slow toke. He glanced at Dewey, smirking and rolling his eyes, but Dewey didn't look up, was studying his fingers. He looked kind of sad. *Party pooper.*

"They've been playing around here for about twenty years," said Shannon. "Beerflesh has." He realized the girl was making him a little nervous, too. He wasn't as bad as Dew, but he wasn't sure he was coming across all that well to her. Losing his old magic touch, maybe. *Just act confident, that's the key.*

"Wow," she said. "Twenty years." Long time to her.

Shannon got bolder. "So what about you? Where are you from, babydoll? May I ask."

"Yes, but pleeeease don't call me babydoll." She touched Dewey's shoulder with the back of her hand, he jumped again, though not as high, and she handed him the joint.

"Or," she said, "I might have to start calling you Daddy." He looked in the mirror. She smiled back at him in that knowing way again.

"My apologizes. So, you're from where?"

"Different places," she said.

50

"Now, that's a good answer. Huh, Dew?" Dewey nodded slightly, didn't chime in.

"Not from around here," she said, yawning, tapping her mouth with her hand.

"You all tuckered out?" said Shannon.

"Wha-aat?"

"Tired?"

"Oh, I thought you said something else. Yeah, I'm tired. Can I sleep back here?"

"Say, man," said Dewey in a low voice, "I hate to ask, but are we still going to pick up Roni?"

"I'm thinkin' it's way too late. I bet she went home." He was keeping his voice a bit low, too. It kind of annoyed him that he was.

"I kind of think we should stop there anyway, just in case."

Now, who the fuck was Dew to advise Shannon about his marriage? When did he ever have a girlfriend that lasted more than a few months, even? He pretended that Alta chick he was fucking for a minute two years ago was still an item, but obviously he never heard from her anymore.

"She won't be there."

"Okay then," said Dewey, like he didn't give a fuck about anything anymore. Christ, it wasn't his problem. The real deal was, what was he going to do with this fabulous babe? He looked in the rearview again. She had her eyes closed now, breathing deep and slow, looked like she was dead asleep.

"Hey, are you asleep back there?"

"Man, leave her be, she's tired," said Dewey.

"No no, I'm awake." She shuffled around, finding a new backseat sleeping position.

"Okay, babyd—I mean, Sky. But go ahead and catch some z's if you feel like it."

Dewey looked at him funny again. *What's wrong now? He didn't like "babydoll" either?*

"This is a weird car," said Sky.

"It's not weird, just old. It's a T-Bird. 1968 four-door coupe," said Shannon. "A classic."

"Wow," she said. "It's so big. Like a boat. Where'd you get it?"

"It belongs to a buddy of mine." He didn't feel like explaining it to her, about how he'd been using it for something like six months now, since the guy's wife left him and he got all dog-depressed.

Staying home alone and drinking all day. Todd made Dewey look like *Mr. Roger's Neighborhood.*

But hey, that gave him an idea. Todd. That was a place where he could put her tonight. Yeah, that was actually a great idea!

In fact, she might even be just what Todd needed to break out of his blues. If you asked him up front if he wanted to meet some girl, he'd say no, but if you asked if he'd let her crash there because she didn't have a place, he might say yes, like he didn't give a fuck, but he might really like the idea. Plus, when he'd been around her for a while, maybe she would get to him and he'd start getting human again.

Plus, she definitely seemed like it wouldn't take much to get her to fuck.

Might be a great fucking thing to do for old Todd. Pay him back for using the T-Bird all these months, even, especially since Shannon really hoped to use it for a little while longer, until worm took off and the money got decent. Oh, and for making worm for him too, since it had really been Dewey's idea after he read that it was getting popular around the country in some article in *Horror Garage* magazine.

And if it turned out Todd wasn't interested, because of the girl in the woods and all, but he let her stay for a night, then maybe Shannon would feel hornier tomorrow, could go back and pick her up and take her somewhere else. Like, to a motel. And if he did that, he'd at least have tried to do a good turn for his unfortunate buddy first.

Then there was Dewey, but, forget him. He wasn't going to do anything with her, even if he'd like to.

They probably should stop at the Limbo first, though, like Dewey said. Roni will have split, but that way he could tell her he did stop and she wasn't there. Plus he could call home from there, and that might chill her out some. Then they could go to Todd's with the chick. Try to call Todd from the Limbo, too, though he didn't always answer his phone.

"Okay, let's head for the Limbo," he said to Dewey. He checked the mirror, looked like Sky had drifted off again.

"The Limbo, now?" said Dewey. He lowered his voice. "I mean, first we gotta do something with," he motioned, pointing his thumb over his shoulder.

"A minute ago you wanted to go there," said Shannon.

"That was because—" Dewey groaned. "Never mind. What if Roni is still there?"

"She won't be. Shit, man, don't worry about every little fucking

52

thing, okay? Everything's cool. Let me do the worrying."

Dewey sighed audibly as Shannon turned off the exit, said nothing more. *Christ*, Shannon thought, *might as well have Dewey's grandma as a running buddy.*

8

TODD AT HOME, READING

Todd was reading further in the *Plan 666* book.

    Behind the rise of the three interrelated cult groups Apocalypsis Ordine Angelorum, the Kindred and Paradise Threshold lies the mysterious figure of Alberic Crabtree, Jamaican occultist, musician, and for a while, soft-drink entrepreneur based in New Orleans and deeply involved with the afrocentric culture of Voudou. Crabtree, who bitterly disavowed A.O.A. and likely would have done the same with the Kindred and Paradise Threshold had he lived to see them, also served as an inspiration to certain filmmakers active in the horror genre, though in his voluminous and largely arcane writing he is said to have displayed no interest whatsoever in the cinema. The most notable instance was of the tragic and controversial Italian auteur, Sabatino Scalabrino, whose descent into madness accompanied his increasing involvement with Crabtreeite doctrine.

    Another devoted follower, for a time, was Delbert Wingdale, alleged alien-spaceship abductee who founded the once greatly popular Kindred group, ostensibly Christian yet focused on a mission of sexual liberation, until his expulsion by the usurper, Myron Richard Grossman, who himself came to be known to the Kindred faithful as "Daddy Dickie" prior to his own conviction and incarceration for child molestation and kidnapping.

Following Wingdale's excommunication at Grossman's orders, he went on to found the tiny, still-more bizarre ufology sect, Paradise Threshold, best known for their conviction that psilocybin mushrooms were actually highly evolved and intelligent intergalactic travelers on a mission to bring spiritual enlightenment to all the inhabited planets of the universe, a concept apparently derived in part from that of the Eucharist . . .

This didn't make much sense to Todd, but it was depressing to read anyway because it reminded him of all of Clare's crazy bullshit that had fucked up their marriage. Or had it?

The big problem with his marriage, really, had been Clare's refusal to fuck after she had the miscarriage. He understood maybe she was afraid of getting pregnant again, but they could have dealt with that. It was that she took it further, said she was against reproducing before the coming return of the Alien Christ from outer space with his army of Niffs, or something like that. But when he argued against that, said they could practice birth control, that it wasn't the only problem, it was that he was too rough in bed. He always had been and was getting worse. He scared her, she said. That was bullshit. Wasn't it?

If they'd had a real marriage and were having sex, the whole episode with Lenore wouldn't have happened. Or would it have? He didn't do anything to her except fuck her. Did he?

Everything had been so strange and fucked up ever since that night.

He looked down at his arm, at his tattoo. It was of a naked girl in a cocktail glass, with angel's wings and bright red hair. That red was the only color in it. He had insisted on red at the tattoo parlor, though the sample had an angel with blonde hair. That was the real—immediate, anyway—reason Clare had left. When he'd come home with the tattoo. Unhinged as she was by then, she knew there was something real significant about it.

9

DEWEY AND SHANNON BACK AT THE LIMBO

Dewey was more than ready to get home and go to bed. What a stupidly fucked-up night it had been. First, sitting around waiting for drunk and scroungy Todd to get the batch of worm done in his really filthy house while the grossest porn movies he'd ever seen played endlessly on his TV. What was that line about porn somebody came up with? Watching for ten minutes makes you want to fuck, an hour makes you never want to fuck again. In Dewey's own case, he'd probably never fuck again anyway.

Then, afterwards, going to the Grasso to meet those kids Shannon was going to sell worm to when it was obviously the wrong place and him picking up this out-of-it chick with hair just like the one in the woods only not Asian and, though it didn't look like Shannon was planning on taking her somewhere and fucking her himself, they'd ended up back at the Limbo, with Roni long gone hours after Shannon was supposed to pick her up.

The chick, Sky, stayed in the back of the car, sleeping. Soon as they came through the door, Heather ran up and eagerly explained

Roni had left at least an hour before, pointedly adding she'd looked really upset that Shannon hadn't shown up. Fred told her to hush and he and Shannon to order one drink and drink it fast because they were closing promptly at two a.m. Shannon said he had to use the phone and hit Dewey up for a quarter. The TV showed that evangelist show Fred was always watching, the old coot who always rattled on about how the Antichrist was already lurking around, getting ready to spring, and after the ensuing apocalypse, everybody would end up in Hell except himself and his loyal viewers.

Shannon came back to the table from the phone. "You got another quarter? Now I gotta call Roni."

"I thought you just did."

"No, I called Todd first, but he didn't answer."

"Why'd you call him?"

"'Cause I'm thinking that's where we can drop off Sky for now."

Dewey was so taken aback he didn't answer for a minute. "Drop her off at Todd's?" He was incredulous.

"Yeah. I figure he could put her up for a while, see what happens."

"See what happens?"

"Yeah." Shannon laughed. "Man, what are you so uptight about?"

"You know Todd's all burned out over what happened to that last stoned chick we picked up. This one's hair even looks the same."

"Fuck no, it doesn't. She's white."

"I'm talking about their red hair."

"That girl didn't really have red hair, she was a chink."

"But he thinks that girl—"

"I know, he thought she died or some shit, but that didn't happen. She got up and left, man, that's all."

"Without her clothes?"

"Yeah, whatever. Stranger things have happened."

"But that's why Todd—" He noticed Heather standing at the bar, watching and listening, and lowered his voice. "That's why fucking Todd is all depressed and withdrawn and shit, because he thinks that girl ODed or something while he was fucking her. He said she wasn't breathing."

"He was flipped out himself," said Shannon. "I don't think he even thinks that anymore. You're the only one who's worried about it. Todd's just bummed out about Clare."

"He might be upset about both," said Dewey. "He acted like—"

"Man, you know what? I know him better than you do. It's about

Clare. So, he might like to have a little female companionship for a day or so. And if he really likes her, you know, as far as I'm concerned, he can keep her for a while."

"He can keep her? She's yours to give away?"

"Man, what the fuck are you, Gloria Steinem or some shit? If the chick doesn't want to do it, she won't."

"Is this about the car?"

"What do you mean, the car? Look, man, they're going to toss us out of here in a minute. Fred wants to go home."

"I want to go home too," called out Heather, standing with her arms folded. Fred must have been in the back, putting stuff away for the night.

"See, she wants to go home too. I need another quarter to call Ron. You got a quarter?"

"If Todd didn't answer, why do you need another quarter?"

"What do you mean?"

"You should have gotten your quarter back."

"Oh. Yeah, I guess you're right. Must be in the coin drop." Shannon stepped back over to the phone while Dewey shook his head until he noticed Heather watching him.

Shannon was at the payphone, dialing, finished, stood there with the headset at his ear. Apparently the phone was just ringing, since Shannon wasn't saying anything. Dewey glanced out the front window, saw somebody in the parking lot by the car looking in the back window at the backseat where the girl was lying. Christ, it was Jaime Tales.

"Hey, Shan, c'mere."

Shannon turned. "What?"

"Jaime Tales is out there fucking with your car. He's checking out the chick." Heather, he noticed, perked up at the word "chick."

"Are you shittin' me?" He hung up the phone, dashed over to the window. "Motherfucker!"

Shannon ran out the door. "*Hey Jaime, what's the problem, asswipe?*" he yelled. Jaime looked up, startled, dashed away real fast, across the street and around the gas station on the other side, with Shannon in pursuit.

Fred came back from the kitchen. "What's going on out here? What's all this yellin' and profanity?"

Still watching the action outside, Dewey saw Shannon look into the back window of the car himself. He'd let Jaime run off without bothering to chase him. He headed back to the Limbo, pushed the door hard and came in.

"He didn't wake her up, she's still asleep back there." Shannon sat down at the table with Dewey, sighing. "Asshole. Jesus." Heather, behind the bar, was wide-eyed. *Well, the whole town will know now.*

"It's two, we're closed," said Fred, crossing his arms. "You can't take them beers with you. Goodnight."

"Yeah, right," said Shannon. "C'mon, Dew." They stood up.

"Hope Roni got home okay," Heather said as Shannon and Dewey headed for the door.

"You just be quiet," said Fred.

10

TODD AT HOME, REMEMBERING

The phone rang, but Todd didn't answer it. Must be a wrong number, and besides, he was preoccupied. That fateful evening the year before unreeled in his mind like a movie he might have watched on video. In fact, some of it was just like porn, but uglier.

He leafed through the book until some familiar words in a passage caught his eye.

The impetus for Wingdale's break with Crabtree remains mysterious, but in later years was said to have to do, oddly enough, with Crabtree's former role as the manufacturer and promoter of Louisiana Bald Cat sarsaparilla in New Orleans back in the '20s. While the drink was alleged to bear an aphrodisiac effect, which probably accounted for its temporary popularity in New Orleans and environs, the only part of the country in which it was readily available, Wingdale claimed that a far more sinister intent lay behind it, especially in a form Wingdale termed "Verum Deus," which may or may not have been a highly concentrated variant of the beverage made up of the same elements, though what these were in the first place remains unknown.

In Wingdale's account, Verum Deus eventually reduced a user to a mentally primitive Id-like state that would allow a sophisticated person to control their minds, in a fashion reminiscent of the popular conception of voodooistic zombies. No evidence has been found that such an effect or project on Crabtree's part ever truly existed, and Wingdale's reputation for exaggeration and outright fabrication does nothing to bolster his credibility on the matter . . .

Huh. Verum Deus was what Hobie said the recipe was for, though everybody called it worm. Was it really the same thing?

The whole business with Lenore had started with that worm shit, back when Hobie had first gotten the theater in the settlement from his parents dying in a cruise ship accident. Hobie had come up with the stuff for it, that Bald Cat, and the recipe he found on some internet newsgroup about this Crabtree fucker he got all interested in because Sabatino Scalabrino liked him. It was a night when Shannon, Dewey and Hobie had gotten together at Todd's to play poker. Clare wasn't around, hadn't left town yet, but had been hard to get along with and was spending a lot of time at her mom's. They were waiting for Hobie to show up, sitting at the table drinking beer and fucking around, talking about the mural Todd was supposed to paint on the side of the building. Shannon seemed interested, but Dewey wasn't saying much. Not that Todd cared what Dewey thought.

Shannon asked what kind of movies they were going to show. "Hope it's not going to be that arty shit." He'd said before he thought Hobie and Todd had too much of that at their video store.

"He'll come up with something else to be into after he gets tired of running the theater. That's going to be a bigger hassle than a video shop."

"I think he already has with this new drug he's come up with," said Todd.

"This isn't meth, right, it's something else?"

"It's a drug made out of some old kind of sarsaparilla," said Todd.

"Out of what?"

"It's like an old-fashioned soft drink, got something to do with voodoo."

"Voodoo? You serious?"

"Yeah, it's called Bald Cat. Louisiana Old-Fashioned Bald Cat Sarsaparilla. They stopped making it in the 1920s or something, but Hobie found a place to order it from with his home computer. It's some shop in New Orleans where you can buy cats' bones and all kinds of shit. You know how he's into all that."

"From the '20s? You mean it's real old, the original shit in old bottles?"

"I guess it's fermented or something. That's why you can use it to make this drug."

"You drink this shit, when it's that old?" Shannon made a grossed-out face.

"The finished product is kind of like candy, you eat it. Looks kinda like gummy worms."

"You *eat* it? It sounds hideous. Have you done this shit?"

"Nope."

"You going to?"

"I don't know."

"Well, fuck old Hobag and his devil dope," said Shannon. "Are we gonna play poker or not?"

"Sure," said Dewey, but everyone kept lying around, watching the porn video Todd had on, all with relative indifference except Dewey, who seemed to be sweating a little.

They had just begun to play poker when Hobie finally showed up about a half hour later, after they'd pretty much given up on him. He was acting real cheerful. Soon as he was in the door, he pulled a large plastic zip-lock bag out of his coat with some pinkish substance in it, shook it.

"Anybody want to sample some Verum Deus?" he said. "I should warn, I'm not talking about an ordinary high."

"What you call it?"

"Verum Deus, is how it's known. Very big with the cogniscenti out on the West Coast."

"Who is the, what you say? What you talkin' 'bout, boy?" Shannon stretched and yawned. "Is this the shit made from Dr. Pepper or, what was it?"

Hobie laughed. "Never mind that, just try it. It's some heavy shit. It's said by some to bring out a person's essential nature."

"Doesn't sound like a good thing to me," said Shannon.

"It's definitely an adventure, and not for the timid. The recipe is quite difficult. Isn't it, Todd? Todd, of course, actually made it."

"Yeah," said Todd. "I mean, I made it. I don't know whether it's, what did you say? Heavy shit?"

"He got you to make it?" Shannon shook his head. "Then you gave it all to him, or what?"

"Yeah," said Todd. "I'm not really that . . ." He shrugged.

"Todd's the chemist around here," said Hobie. "I'm just the visionary."

"I wouldn't call it chemistry, exactly," said Todd.

"I don't necessarily like 'heavy shit,'" said Shannon. "What is it, like acid? I don't do acid."

"There's really nothing to compare it to," said Hobie.

"This is that seventy-year-old shit Todd was telling us about?"

"Actually, I have no idea how old it is."

"Doesn't sound like it's safe if it's seventy years old, man."

"I've tried it several times myself, no ill effects whatsoever," said Hobie.

"I'm not taking any," said Dewey, but Todd figured he would if Shannon did.

"Where'd you find this shit again?"

"I got the recipe some time back from some literature put out by the Apocalypsis Ordine Angelorum group."

"The who?" said Shannon.

"An occult group. I didn't even think it was a real thing because the main ingredient was this product from a long-defunct company in New Orleans, but lo and behold, I found some online. It's—"

"Apoca-what?" said Todd. "You didn't tell me that part. Isn't that some Satanist group or something? I think Clare mentioned them sometime." He couldn't remember, there was so much weird shit she talked about anymore.

"They're a Crabtreeite group from the West Coast," said Hobie. "Apparently they got involved in some shenanigans back in the '60s, but I understand today they're pretty benign."

"Oh, that's reassuring," said Shannon. "Not carving up pregnant sex symbols anymore, huh?"

Hobie laughed. "Nothing like that." He sat down in Todd's rocking chair near the TV.

Shannon got up, reached for the bag. "Looks kind of like fucking worms. You sure some flies didn't lay eggs in here? You supposed to eat it?"

"Of course."

"You sure? You just eat it?"

"Correct."

"How much?"

"A spoonful," said Hobie, pulling a spoon from his pocket.

"Wow, you're all prepared."

Hobie dipped into the stuff, pulled a spoonful and put it in his mouth.

"I'm not using the same fucking spoon as you," said Shannon.

"Okay, I'll get some spoons," said Todd, going into the kitchen.

When he returned, Shannon dipped in and tried it, and then Todd did as well. Dewey, as Todd expected, did too, since Shannon had, though he acted reluctant about it.

"Jeez, it tastes bitter, doesn't it?" said Shannon. "I thought it would be sweet like pop."

"Well, are we going to play poker or what?" said Dewey.

"I doubt that this game will last," said Hobie. "It's supposed to take effect quite quickly."

"What'd you mean, s'posed to? I thought you already took some."

"I did, but it was from a different batch."

"Same shit, though, right?"

"Certainly."

They went on playing poker, for small stakes since Shannon insisted he couldn't play unless it was for money. Before too long, Todd noticed everyone was getting pretty quiet, and he himself couldn't concentrate on the cards. In fact, the game had broken down completely, and they were just sitting around the table motionlessly, staring at each other, apparently all of them with their minds sludged considerably.

Todd looked at each face, judging that Hobe appeared to be the most impaired. An ambiguous section of time passed. Todd thought about getting up, but didn't. Eventually he started to feel somewhat energized, almost with a start.

Just then, he saw that Dewey had the top off the container of stuff, Verum whatever, and was peering into it. He said, "Jesus fuck, this shit is moving. It's worms! It's live worms!"

Shannon had seemed really out of it, but snapped alert suddenly. "Say what? Lemme see that shit."

"Goddamn, you're right! Fuckin' Hobag, what the fuck—"

He jumped up, grabbed him by the shoulder and shook him.

Todd picked up the bag, opened it. It didn't look to him like they were moving at all, but he didn't say anything.

"Hold it, Shannon, look at him," said Todd. "He's still out if it. Way out if it."

"Fucker. I hope he never comes down. When he does, we oughta kick his ass. Makin' us eat live worms."

"They're not moving," said Todd. "Look." He held open the bag. Shannon looked for a long moment. "Okay, maybe they're not."

"Actually, I'm starting to feel pretty good," said Todd.

"Whatever," said Shannon. "Actually, I don't feel that bad either. Surprised I'm not puking. You wanna go out?"

"Yeah, I do," said Dewey. "Let's go."

"You don't wanna finish this game?"

"What game?"

"What about Hobie?" They looked over at him. He appeared to be in a trance, or at least deeply preoccupied.

"Fuck him. Leave him here."

"Shouldn't we, like, lie him down on the couch or something?" said Dewey.

"Naw, let him sit there," said Shannon. "He looks comfy." With that, they left. There was a strange sense of energy in the air.

Outside, Shannon said, "Yo, Todd, can I drive your ride? I like to drive that fuckin' thing." Meaning his car, the '68 Thunderbird.

"Sure, go ahead." Todd didn't like to drive it that much anyway, found it hard to steer, kind of like what he figured it must be like to steer a yacht. Besides, Shannon could be like a little kid about stuff like that.

"How come Hobie got all nodded out on this stuff?" said Dewey.

"He always reacts some weird way to shit," said Shannon. "'Member how back when we first got him to smoke pot, he took a hit, got all frantic and fell to the floor thrashing around?"

"Yeah, I remember. Had a panic attack. He said 'I'm freaking out!'"

"Then a couple years ago he said he didn't remember that ever happening."

"He said that longer than a couple years ago."

"Course, you know what his real problem is?"

"I know what you think it is," said Todd. "It is. He hates being a faggot. Wants to like girls, but he doesn't."

"Could be, I dunno," said Dewey. He was going to add that Hobie obviously liked Roni a lot, but thought better of it. Not a good subject to bring up with Shannon. "Where we going? Anywhere?"

"Didn't somebody say something about a strip joint?" said Todd, though no one had.

"Huh! I don't think so, but that's funny, 'cause that's just what I was thinking," said Shannon. "You know what I really wanna do? See some pussy. Not in movies. The live stuff."

"That sounds okay," said Dewey. It was somewhat out of character for him to say he actually wanted to do something.

"Let me rephrase that," said Shannon. "I wanna *smell* some pussy. Like, at a titty bar, a good sleazy one where the bitches put it in your face. I could go for that about now."

"Well, we could go to Yum-Yums," said Todd. This was a nude dancing bar they'd gone to a few times years before.

"Is that even still around? I thought it closed," said Dewey.

"I dunno. Let's go out there and see." It was evening, just getting to be dark out.

They rode on, Shannon talking about girls at Yum-Yums they'd seen years before. "Remember that one little bitch, with the blue hair? She said her name was 'Fantasy.'"

"Let's hope she's not still there, she'll be long in the tooth now," said Todd.

"Aw, you're just a sexist, man," said Shannon.

"Shelf life is short for strippers," said Todd. "They're like produce."

"Uh, say, you guys. Don't look now, guess who's following us," said Dewey.

"What, the pigs?" said Shannon, turning around in his seat to look.

"Nope. Jaime Tales, on a bike. He's hanging back about a block, probably thinks we don't see him."

Todd laughed, turned around too. "Really, is that him way back there?"

"Yeah, look at his jacket," said Dewey. "Who else wears a green plaid jacket?"

"Fuckin' narc, I swear to God." Shannon did a screeching u-turn, which Todd thought was not good for the old Thunderbird at all, but he didn't say anything. Heading toward him, it was Jaime, all right.

As they passed him in the other direction, Shannon yelled at Jaime, "Hey, officer, what's the charge?" but Jaime looked away and pumped on ahead. Shannon made another u-turn, sped up and swerved close to Jaime. Startled, he rolled to the side of the road and fell off his bike into the gravel.

"Christ, don't run him over, man," said Todd.

"You need to learn to ride that fuckin' bike, Tales, you fuckin' dumbass moron!" Shannon yelled out the window, and zoomed on.

That seemed to be the end of Jaime's pursuit of them. They drove on.

"I still think it's closed. That Yum-Yums place," said Dewey.

"Aw, you're a crepe-hanger," said Shannon. "That's what my mom used to call people who were negative, crepe-hangers."

After a couple minutes, Todd looked back and saw Jaime, up and riding again and still following, from a farther distance back. He didn't say anything about it, though. He was feeling pretty frisky too but didn't want them to do anything really irresponsible because Shannon tended to get wild, and he knew that Dewey, though he'd fret, would go along with whatever Shannon wanted to do.

They came upon Yum-Yums. The sign for it was still up, but it was dark and appeared definitely closed. Looked like it had been for a while, in fact. The sign, a big pair of googly eyes with cameos of dancing girls around it, was dingy with grime and had a jagged hole, as though someone had broken it with a thrown rock.

However, they all saw at once, there was a girl standing right in front of the place, head down, going through her purse. She wore a short red dress and green hose, and had nice legs. Her long, stringy hair, oddly, was a bright shade of red, like a Raggedy Ann doll. When she raised her head, she appeared to have slanted Asian eyes.

"Hey, let's pick up that hooker," said Shannon.

"I dunno, man," said Dewey. "She's Chinese, isn't she?" Todd laughed, not knowing why Dewey saying that seemed funny.

The girl paid no attention as they drove up. "Hey, honey?" called Shannon.

Some moments passed before she answered. "What?" she said, sounding exasperated.

"What's the problem? You look cold."

"I am cold and I can't find my fucking money."

"Not a hooker," said Todd, thinking aloud.

"What you need money for?" said Shannon.

"To call a fucking cab! What else?"

"You don't need a cab. You can come with us."

"Yeah, right," she said. "Where you gonna take me?" She struck a pose, curving her figure with her hip thrust out and a fist on it, scowling as if defiantly.

Todd thought, but didn't say, that maybe she was a hooker after all.

"Wherever, c'mon," said Shannon.

She groaned. "All right, beats freezing out here." She got into the back seat, next to Todd, and they drove off. She was kind of cute and smelled of perfume.

"So, what you been up to this evening?" asked Shannon, smirking.

"I went on a date with this asshole, and he was so fucking boring I had to ditch him."

"You ditched him?"

"We were at a restaurant, he was acting all nervous and stupid and telling me about his dad's law firm, so I told him I was going to the ladies' room, left out the back. I mean, I could tell he was going to bore me stiff all evening, but then he wouldn't even be a good fuck."

It got quiet in the car, until Todd laughed. Then they all laughed.

"What's so funny," the girl said, deadpan.

"Nothing," said Todd, and then it occurred to him, in fact, it wasn't funny. Close up, the girl's pupils, in those lovely Asian eyes, were huge. She was real stoned, almost as stoned as Hobie had been.

"You guys are fucking silly," she said.

"Maybe, but you'll find we're not boring like that guy you dumped," said Shannon.

"Yeah? You act like you're all wired up."

"Yeah, kind of. You wanna get that way too?"

She already was, in some kind of way, but said, "On what?"

"On this shit were doing," said Shannon.

"What the fuck, it's Saturday night." Actually, it was Sunday, but no one pointed this out.

"We don't have any with us," said Dewey. "It's back at Todd's."

"Oh yeah, you're right," said Shannon. "Fuck a duck."

"Well, fuck you too then," said the girl. This cracked up the bunch of them.

"So where are we going?"

"That depends on where the young lady would like to go," said Shannon. "Where would you like to go? Excuse me, young lady?"

She looked dazed and didn't respond. She leaned her head on Todd's shoulder, put her hand on his thigh.

"Yoo-hoo," said Shannon. "Young lady?"

"She looks passed out, I think," said Dewey.

Todd was suddenly so horny it was like he had to take a piss real bad. "Let's take her out to the woods," said Todd. "Right over there."

"Are you serious?"

"Yes!"

"Okay, boss. Damn." Shannon turned off the road.

"Hey, man, I'm not sure we oughta do this," said Dewey.

"You don't wanna disappoint our guest, do you?" said Shannon. "We don't want to bore her."

Todd noticed that she wore a bracelet on her wrist that said Lenore. He began opening her blouse. She wore, they all saw, a pink push-up brassiere. Todd put his hand under one cup of it . . .

Todd's reverie was interrupted by a knock at the door.

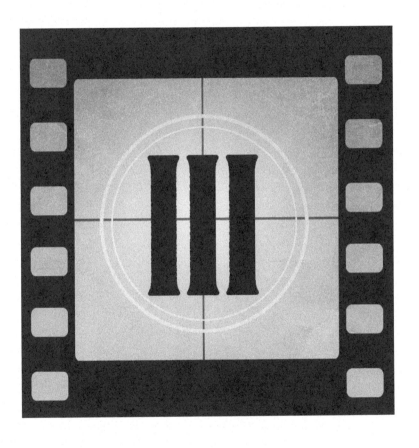

11

JAMIE AT HOME

It was the small hours of the morning when Jaime got back to his home in the upper story of the theater. The only way to get there that he knew of was to go up the fire escape in the back, which had a missing section in its center, so that he had to reach up, grab the rung of a metal ladder to pull himself up, a bit hazardously, and scramble onto a platform that led to the unlatched window he used as an entrance. There was a staircase inside he could use—that's how he'd discovered the apartment up there in the first place, just looking around up there one day—but he figured it was safer to just climb through the window.

The stench of the stopped-up toilet hit him in the face as soon as he came through the window, despite the cold. It wasn't like anyone ever came to visit, but it was making him feel kind of sick, especially in the first few minutes he'd be there. Besides, he was worried more and more that people downstairs would notice it and find out he was staying up there.

Darn, he was getting that weird little pain in his chest again.

Happened when he was tired out, it seemed like.

Picking up his camper's light he left just inside the window, he stepped over to the little broom closet where the toilet was located, pinching his nose closed with his fingers. Gosh, it was rank. The mix of his shit and piss in the toilet, and some under it that was hardened and black and may have been there for years, wouldn't go down at all, and the flush handle was missing and there hadn't been any water in it at all ever since the renovation a few months ago. There was an old plunger on the floor of the closet, though, and out of desperation, he decided to use it to try to push the mess down the hole.

The condition of the place wasn't really that different from the way his family's house had been, pretty dilapidated and disordered and stinky, except, back there, he didn't have any privacy at all. He'd always slept with his little sister, Dawnie, until she got hit by a car at age seven and a half, because they were the closest in age, and that wasn't in a regular bed, but on the old cracked-up Bark-o-Lounger that his mother always called Pappaw Hardwick's chair because they'd gotten it from his house when he died. After Dawnie got run over, he'd had to sleep with Bud Junior and Marlon, who sometimes would push him out on the floor, sometimes on purpose and sometimes just in thrashing around, while Maamaw got Pappaw's chair so Mom wouldn't have to sleep with her anymore and could have company over when she wanted to.

That was around the time things got really bad with Marlon and Bud, who tended to use Jaime as a punching bag and twist doll, at first until he'd cry "uncle" but later until he'd weep and scream, and eventually they wouldn't even stop at that unless somebody intervened. Mom would yell because she didn't want to hear "that fuckin' racket" and sometimes would slap him as well as his brothers for it. If Mom wasn't around when it happened, Maamaw would yell at them and sometimes even lock herself and Jaime into Mom's bedroom so they couldn't get at him.

He put the plunger in the toilet and pushed. The putrid mix of offal spurted up the sides of the toilet bowl and over onto the floor. *Dammit!*

Maamaw had really been the only one in the family who was ever nice to him, not only trying to protect him from his brothers but sometimes holding him on her lap, bouncing him around and saying he was "a li'l darlin'" and "my best grandbaby," though she'd do and say the same with Dawnie sometimes too.

74

Even Dawnie he didn't get along with that well. They'd play together sometimes, but she'd easily get enraged and bite him and claw his face when he had some toy she wanted to play with, or something like that.

It was bad after Bud's accident and he was living at home. He looked so awful Jaime was more scared of him than ever. Then he died, and Dawnie got run over, and Maamaw got sick and sent to the Medicaid nursing home where, to Jaime's dismay, she got so she didn't even recognize him or anybody else in the family, and Marlon moved out and Cheryl Sue had a fight with her friend she lived with and moved back in. Jaime had stayed just with Mom, and though they didn't get along and there was always some kind of trouble going on, that was the best time as far as he was concerned.

But after Maamaw died and Marlon drove into the quarry and died too, Ma got so she kept inviting people to live with them. First came Violet, who had three kids with "developmental disabilities," according to their high-strung mother, and were no fun to be around. Then, after Cheryl Sue got mad at Mom and she and Violet and the kids left, Mom got her a new young boyfriend called Monkey who was a biker and all his buddies started living there, and Monkey kept threatening Jaime and accusing him of messing with his bike though he never went near the thing, and Mom would always take Monkey's side, so he finally decided to go out on his own, though he didn't exactly have a place to live. He'd really been lucky to find the apartment upstairs in the theater, but now that arrangement was threatened by the toilet problem.

Looking for something to wipe off the fouled plunger with, Jaime found there was a real fancy old-fashioned-looking faucet in the bottom of the wall beside where the plunger had been. He tried turning this and was surprised it not only moved easily but the sound of briskly running water started up. Checking the water tank behind the toilet, which itself was old-fashioned and huge, Jaime was delighted to see it start to fill.

The tank filled almost to the brim, and Jaime was about to turn it off before it spilled over, when it gurgled loudly and the toilet bowl itself began to fill. *Great!* He enthusiastically picked up the plunger again to help push the mess down the hole, but after a couple of hard plunges, he heard a loud crack, and all the water and much of the mess in the bowl rushed away, and the water in the tank after it. Puzzled and not entirely sure this was a good thing, Jaime turned the knob shut. There was, he thought, a sound like rain coming from outside but, checking the window, the dark sky was clear.

Uh oh, Jaime thought. All the sudden he had a real bad feeling about it.

12

TODD MEETS SKY

Todd opened the door to see Shannon standing there with a girl. A beautiful girl, twenty or so, with long bright-red hair, a white dress and a black leather jacket. Bright red hair, like Raggedy Ann and like Lenore.

"Hey, dude," said Shannon, grinning and stepping inside without being invited. The girl stood still, looking straight at Todd, as if puzzled and trying to remember him from somewhere. He'd definitely never seen her before. "C'mon in, kid," said Shannon, reaching back for her hand, leading her forward. Todd waited for Shannon to introduce her, but he didn't. He was embarrassed at the state of his place and at his own appearance, dressed in his bathrobe with a t-shirt underneath it, both of which he'd had on for some days, and his own hair was likely in bird's nest condition.

"Hey," said Todd. "Have a—" He was about to say "Have a seat," but Shannon had already sat on the sofa, which was cluttered with dirty laundry Todd had accumulated there a few days ago, intending to take it down to the basement to wash it.

"Sorry the place is a mess," he said. The girl was still standing there, looking intently, it seemed, at Todd. The red hair was still getting him.

"Typical bachelor housekeeping," said Shannon, grinning. "Looks like my old place. Hey, girl, sit here," said Shannon, grabbing a bunch of the clothes and looking around for a place to put them. Todd came up and took them from him, as if apologetically, and placed them on the floor beside an armchair that he then sat down in.

"Dew's out in the car," said Shannon. "He's wiped out. Long night."

"Huh," said Todd.

The girl sat next to Shannon, close, looked around with a blank expression, turned and looked straight at Todd again. He was surprised when she spoke.

"Can I use your bathroom?"

"Sure," said Todd, and Shannon nodded. "Yeah, that's good." *That's good?* Todd pointed out where the bathroom was, first door on the left down the hallway, and she went, leaving him and Shannon alone.

"I tried to call you on the phone a while ago," said Shannon, "but no answer."

"Yeah. What's going on?" he asked in a low voice.

"I wondered if you'd do me a favor."

"Okay." He nodded in the direction the girl had gone, puzzled Shannon could mean anything to do with her.

"Yeah, her. She needs a spot. Plus, I figured maybe you could use some company."

Todd stared at him for a moment, until Shannon shrugged comically, raising his shoulders and spreading out his hands. At that, Todd laughed incredulously.

"Well, man, we were trying to think of a place for her to crash, so, I figured here might work out." He took out a pack of cigarettes, put one in his mouth and lit up.

"Where'd she come from?"

"I ran into her tonight at the Grasso, and she's a real nice girl and all. You'd like her. I thought about you right away when this came up, 'cause I thought you might, you know, like her and stuff."

"She's not a customer, is she?"

"No, no. The customers were no-shows. I'll catch up with 'em, though."

It occurred to Todd his shit-clogged pants were still on the floor of the bathroom. He blanched.

"If you don't want to, though, that's cool," said Shannon, sounding rather disappointed.

"Well. I don't know, man."

"If you don't want to, I can take her back to the Grasso, probably. Well, actually, it's closed. I can't take her home with Roni there, and Dew doesn't really . . ."

Todd heard the toilet flush and the bathroom door opening.

"She can stay here," he said.

"Oh, really?" Shannon grinned. "For a minute I thought you weren't enthused."

"I'm not enthused, but it's okay."

"Awright, great," said Shannon. "I don't think you'll be sorry, man." He laughed, but Todd didn't join in.

The girl stepped back into the room. "Hey, there she is." Shannon looked her over and glanced back at Todd, raising an eyebrow and nodding in comradeship.

She sat beside Shannon. "Can I get a cigarette?" He offered her his pack of Camels. "Oh no, not those again."

"I have some Marlboro Lights," Todd said.

"Oh, really? Great." He jumped up, went into the next room where the TV was and where he usually smoked as well as drank. He found just a crumpled empty pack beside the ashtray, went into the kitchen to get some out of his carton. He wondered what they were saying in the living room. Now, dammit, he was kind of worried she was saying she doesn't want to stay. Not that he really wanted her to, but he also doesn't want to get rejected by a girl like that. Old stuff about girls, from high school and like that. *So stupid*, he thought, returning with the pack and bringing the ashtray and lighter along too.

"Thanks," she said, lighting up, red hair hanging as she lowered her head to the flame.

"Say," said Shannon, "I talked to Todd just now, about the arrangement and all, and it's cool with him if it is with you."

"What is? To stay here?"

Todd felt a pull of dread in his chest. She was going to say no.

"Yeah. You need a place, right?"

"Ummm."

"It's cool, you know. He's safe. He's a gentleman." He leaned forward and slapped Todd on the shoulder, making him wince.

She looked at Todd and smiled, her lips closed, and said nothing.

"Just for, whatever, a few days, or whatever you guys want to do," said Shannon.

"Okay," said the girl. "Thanks." Her face brightened. Her eyes were as green as her hair was red. Todd suppressed a need to clear his throat.

"Awright, well, that worked out then," said Shannon. "Well, man, hey, I gotta split. Roni's going to be wondering where I am and shit." He stood. "So, like, give me a call, you know. You got my number."

"Yeah," said Todd.

"Well, hey," Shannon rose, grinned. "Take it easy. Sky, you behave, sweet thing."

What did he say? Sky? Todd went to the door and opened it. Shannon went out, turned and gave him a thumbs-up before continuing down the walk. Todd thought he might have winked, too, but wasn't sure.

Closing the door, Todd saw that the girl—Sky?—had stretched out and had her eyes closed, her head lying on her arms on the shoulder of the sofa.

"Say," he said, "I'm sorry the place is a wreck like this, I was just going to straighten it up. I wasn't . . ." He was about to say "expecting company," but didn't.

"Oh, don't bother," she said, opening her eyes and smiling at him.

"Could I, umm, get you a pillow?"

"Yes, that would be nice." He'd see what he had in the bedroom. It wouldn't be in a clean pillowcase.

"Oh, say, did Shannon introduce us? My name is Todd."

"Yes, he said that. I'm Sky."

"Sky?"

"Ummm-hmmm," she said sleepily.

"Okay. I'll go get that pillow." He did, and when he returned, she already had her eyes closed. He left it softly on the floor in front of the sofa, sat down and watched her.

Sleeping beauty. But that red hair, so much like Lenore. He fretted. He shouldn't have let her stay.

13

RONI AND SHANNON AT HOME

When she first heard Shannon come through the door, Roni lay in bed awake, quietly seething. She pretended to be asleep. When he came in to look at her, she kept her eyes closed. He went into the next room, to sleep on the sofa, probably. That meant he didn't want to argue with her. She stayed in bed and tried to sleep and did so only a little, lying half-awake until the alarm went off at six.

She got up to take a shower, finished fast and dried her hair with a blow-dryer and got dressed for work. Went into the living room, found him lying on the sofa with his boots still on, which annoyed her further.

"Hey. Slept out here, didn't want to wake you up," he said. "What you doin' up so early?"

"Hobie wants me to come in early because Stella's off."

"Well, fuck him."

"Out late last night, weren't you?"

He sighed. "Yeah. Yeah, I was. Some stuff came up. Sorry about

81

the Limbo, I couldn't make it."

"Something so important came up you couldn't pick me up like you said you would, or even call to tell me—"

He sat up. "Hey, I just couldn't get there. I don't blame you for being pissed, but I couldn't help it."

"Oh, you don't blame me! That's so generous of you."

"I said I'm sorry." He lay back down, put his arm over his eyes.

"You're always sorry. Aren't you going to tell me what came up that was so important you forgot to pick me up, again? Did you have to go meet someone else at the last minute?"

"Yeah, but it wasn't a girl, if that's what you mean."

"I didn't even suggest it was girl, did I? All I did was ask—"

He interrupted with, "Okay, I was supposed to meet these three kids about," he seemed to hesitate, "about a band." He remained pokerfaced.

This admission surprised her. "Three kids?" *Wait a minute, he probably went to the Limbo later and Heather blabbed about those kids showing up while I was there.*

"Yep." He lay back and put his arm over his eyes. This, she knew from experience, was a sign that he was lying.

"But . . . about a band. What do you mean?"

"A band, a music band. You know what a band is."

"Why would you be meeting them about a band?"

"I was going to manage this rock band, make some extra money. You know construction business is down."

"What do you know about managing a band?"

"I've known people in bands and stuff."

"Why didn't you tell me about it?"

"Because I knew you'd sneer at me over it, like you just did."

"So you're going to . . ." she almost growled in frustration. "Where did you even meet these kids in the first place?"

"It doesn't matter because it's not going to work out. They're getting somebody else."

Roni didn't believe this story at all. She was about to ask whether they changed their minds because he didn't show up where he was supposed to, but decided not to. "But it doesn't have to do with dealing drugs or anything, of course."

"Not unless music is drugs."

"Because you used to deal drugs and, like you say, construction is down."

"I did not deal drugs. I was just dealing a little pot sometimes. To my friends."

"Pot is a drug."

"Yeah, sort of. Not much money in it, though."

"No money in dealing pot? That's not what I always hear."

"Not unless you— Oh for Christ's sake. Maybe you think I should deal pot, then. I had you all wrong."

She groaned. "You know, I can't deal with this. I have to go to work." She went into the bedroom, got dressed, came back out and said, "Will you please at least take your boots off if you're going to lay on the couch?"

He groaned, but was sitting up and taking them off as she went out the door without saying goodbye.

14
SKY SCREAMS

Todd sat in the armchair, watching the girl sleep as though viewing an early Andy Warhol movie. He'd gotten dressed in some of the clothes picked from his batch of dirty laundry. It occurred to him this was a strange thing to do, at least for most people. But it was basically similar to his usual activity in the last few months, sitting and watching porn videos on his TV set, not finding them stirring or engaging, but just something to watch. As though the images were dancing flames in a fireplace, and as though he had all the time in the world and no use he wished to make of it. Ordinarily at this hour he would be watching videos and drinking wine, nodding off occasionally. But the presence of a real girl was keeping him awake and alert, if as passive and listless as ever.

It seemed unreal to him that the girl, Sky, was a living thing, three-dimensional and made of flesh. Weird to think if she woke, she would be able to see him as much as he could see her. She was a thing that could be touched and could respond. Funny, at this point, he could hardly imagine that.

She stirred, snuggled her shoulders against the pillow he'd picked up from the floor in the small hours, and breathed deeply in her sleep.

He really ought to take this time while she was sleeping to clean up the place. Get those pants off the bathroom floor, do the laundry, the bedclothes especially. She could have the bed, he could sleep on the sofa, or in his chair. He usually did anyway.

She didn't look much like Lenore, despite the hair. As he remembered her, anyway. Didn't look much like Clare either. Clare was taller, more athletic, and a blonde, with fine hair and light coloring, hard and sleek angles in her face and figure. This girl Sky's flesh was freckled but pale, which seemed to go with red hair and, though easily as alluring, somehow looked softer in texture than Clare's. He wondered if it felt that way as well. She'd make a nice subject for a drawing, or even more, a painting. Not that he felt like trying to make one, it would just be frustrating to try. But he'd like to, if he could do it and be satisfied with the result. Satisfaction, that was always the problem.

Was it because of Clare he didn't try to paint or draw anymore? All his ambition seemed to have dwindled away, ambition that had gotten to be as much a vice as drinking, and as destructive, in its way. His last project, the unfinished, never-really-begun mural for an outside wall at the Mirror, had been his most ambitious ever, though it wasn't even basically his own idea.

It was Hobie, sort of his best friend back in high school, who couldn't draw at all by himself, who had come up with the design for the mural. He'd described it as awkwardly and insistently as Walt Disney was said to have given instruction to his drudges in his animation factory during the making of *Fantasia*. It was to be a medievalesque rendering of the Harrowing of Hell, a phrase Todd had heard but didn't know the meaning of until Hobie explained it. In the Harrowing, Christ descended into Hell for three days following his crucifixion. For what reason, Hobie didn't say, but he visited the suffering and imprisoned spirits there. Todd didn't remember this from Bible school when his religious crackpot parents were alive. He'd never paid much attention there anyway. But Hobie had read about it at some point, in his fixation on religion as a delightfully camp carnival of delusion.

Hobie's vision was to have a glowing Christ figure hanging above the pitiful damned in a cavern with the dimensions and detailing of a cathedral, who would look up at him beseechingly out of a reddened muck, bearing the faces of dead movie stars, with a special emphasis on those associated mainly with horror movies, like Lugosi, Chaney Jr., Peter Lorre, Vincent Price, Paul Naschy, whoever else. For actresses, Hobie had mentioned Evelyn Ankers, Erika Blanc, Yutte Stensgaard, Barboura Morris and Susan Cabot, and of course, Sharon Tate. The Christ figure itself would be Ed Wood Jr. in something like his transvestite gear from *Glen or Glenda*, perhaps a white robe, definitely a blonde wig and make-up.

Todd was willing to try and did want to play a part in the whole endeavor with the theater, though Hobie was doing all the real work. But all he'd managed to finish at the Mirror itself was the white varnished surface to paint on, and that little flying saucer. At home, he'd done a number of preliminary sketches and acrylic tryouts, but was never satisfied with any of it. Hobie had gotten a sizable money settlement some years after his parents were killed in an accident on a cruise ship vacation. His aunt, an attorney, had kept most of the money, but Hobie did okay. He'd been pretty spendthrift about it, first opening a video store along with Todd, then closing that and renting a large abandoned theater in town. He'd advanced Todd a large amount of money for the mural, an insane twenty grand, though it remained unfinished. Todd didn't know when he'd get back to it, maybe never, but had been living off that money for some months. Hobie never called him anymore, so maybe he'd actually forgotten about it. Todd himself had let the whole thing be put off indefinitely and perhaps forever.

Well, maybe he could make money off this worm thing. Though, at some point, he'd have to consult with Hobie about getting some more of that Bald Cat soda pop or whatever it was, the main ingredient. He still had several bottles of it in the basement, but he thought Hobie either had some more or could get some.

Glancing at Sky on the sofa, he noticed she now had her eyes open and was looking at him. Occupied with his thoughts, he hadn't noticed when she'd woken up. She stretched nicely, shook her hair like a mop, and gave a wide yawn ending in a bright smile. How did she keep her teeth so white like that?

"Have you been awake all night?" she asked.

"All night? Why? Is it . . ." The curtains in his place were dark but, looking at the corners of the windows, he saw the first light of dawn had come.

She sat up. "Is it okay if I take a shower?"

"Umm, sure. Just let me, uh, go and do one thing." *Those pants on the floor.* "Umm, make sure there's some soap and all. Just take a minute."

She nodded, and he hurried off to hide the evidence of his bad habits, though it had already been on display. If only he'd known she was coming. But if he had, he probably would have tried to prevent it.

It was still quite a mess, but he didn't have time to clean up. He did put out a fresh bar of soap. Thankfully, there was an unopened one in the cabinet.

He stepped into the next room. "Okay, it's all ready," he said.

"Great," she smiled and jounced off the sofa, unbuttoning her shirt and pulling it off as she went. Her back was bare, no bra. She turned her head and smiled mischievously. "Do you want to take one too? We could shower together."

He paused, surprised. "Uh, how about I take one later. I'm kind of, not ready to take one right now."

She cocked her head, gave him a direct look with those green eyes. "Okay. See you in a bit." Her walk was somewhat slinky, provocative. He probably did need a shower, but, no.

He sat on the sofa in the spot she'd occupied, still very warm from her body, and listened to the shower coming on full. Naked and getting all squeaky clean in there. *Yikes.* What was he going to do? He hadn't been laid since Lenore, didn't even jerk off, even when he watched porn. Did anybody besides him watch porn and never jerk off?

Listening to Sky in the shower, Todd began thinking again of Clare. It was weird how she'd developed these crazy theories so much like the religious stuff she'd been so against when they first met. Clare had been into some hippie and New Age shit before, but she didn't start to get wacky until after the miscarriage, after saying she didn't want to fuck anymore, and then after Lenore.

He picked up the *Plan 666* book, tried to find the part he'd been reading earlier, couldn't. He found this:

. . . Crabtree claimed the concoction allowed for communication with deep psychic forces in the center of the Earth, imprisoned there by a higher civilization from outer space, which he named the Niff, while the prisoners were Gnoomes, and the female humanoid creatures the Gnoomes employed to expand the human race through lust were called the Qwiff. There is some evidence Crabtree had worked as a pimp in his early days in the New Orleans area. His eventual incarceration

in Brushy Mountain State Penitentiary in Tennessee was the result of a conviction under the Mann Act, for transporting underage women across state lines. It was in Brushy Mountain that Crabtree died in 1943, in a supposed suicide by hanging that many observers deem highly suspicious.

In Crabtree's elaborated interpretation, the Qwiff were the original female humans, invented by the Niff to spread their influence across the Earth by causing the human race, originally a primitive but pure genderless species that lived in perfect accord with nature, to at once evolve and decline. Crabtree apparently did not explain in any of his writings how the genderless proto-humans reproduced; one interpretation is that they were initially immortal and only declined into mortality as a consequence of physical lust.

There's some evidence that Wingdale, who'd been diagnosed in his late teens as paranoid schizophrenic and at various times in his earlier life was confined in mental hospitals, had become still more demented in the late period of his leadership of the Kindred, just prior to his forced departure. Developing Crabtree's Qwiff conception further along deeply misogynistic lines, Wingdale alleged that Qwiff kill the men they've seduced by beheading them, and thus somehow steal their mind-essence, to then carry for some ambiguous purpose down into the underworld. These killings, he claimed, were fairly frequent but widespread and thus little noted, but the time would come, shortly before the return of the Alien Christ, when the numbers of Qwiff dispatched would greatly increase. An inspiration for this dark concept was likely the natural practice of the female praying mantis, which bites off the head of her male mate during intercourse and devours his corpse.

In later interpretations, the Qwiff were either sacred prostitutes or sinister seductresses, recruited from the fallen among womankind and rendered as soulless or even literally heartless creatures. A much later interpretation had it that the Qwiff were "retired" by agents of the Gnoomes known as Jaks, who would reclaim their hearts to install them in other, more reliable Qwiffs.

Delbert Wingdale claimed to have been captured by Gnoomes when he pursued a Qwiff named Lily into the underworld, whom he'd engaged as a prostitute after she'd stolen his pants and run away from a hotel room they'd shared in a small town in Louisiana. He emerged eight years later and founded the Kindred organization, claiming to have been liberated from his imprisonment by Christian evangelist Niffs who taught that Christ was himself a revolutionary latter-day Niff who'd come to Earth to redeem the human race who'd suffered so long under the wicked dominance of the Gnoomes, but had been defeated by the Gnoomian forces. The evangelical Niffs, known as Shrooms, had journeyed to Earth themselves as an advanced force of an army the Savior had been assembling for nearly two Earth millennia to do battle with the Gnoomes in a final apocalyptic war for the liberation of humanity . . .

Yep, this was some of that same crazy shit both Hobie and Clare used to talk about. Maybe the book was actually Hobie's and not Clare's.

Clare had always said he was waiting for a girl to come to him and she'd be an angel or an alien, or something—it was some theory of hers. Maybe it was this Qwiff thing. She probably would have said that was what Lenore had been.

He didn't like to think about the last part of the Lenore story, wasn't sure what about it was real and what might have been a hallucination. He didn't even remember it very coherently, as if it had all been a dream. It was in the woods. There had only been moonlight. First Shannon had her on the ground, had gotten her blouse open and her dress pulled up. She didn't have any panties, he remembered that. He wasn't sure whether Shannon was fucking her before he'd somehow noticed Jaime Tales spying on him from behind a tree.

"Fuckin' Tales, you little cocksucker!" he'd raged, and when Jaime ran, Shannon had jumped up, chasing after him, trying to yank up his own pants as he ran. Dewey ran after him, God knows why. Why should Shannon even care that much about Tales watching? He could run him down later if he really wanted to.

Lenore sat up, turned her head and looked at Todd, exasperated. "Can any of you guys actually fuck?" she said.

Challenged, he'd gone to the task, taking the rest of her clothes off and tossing them aside while she struggled teasingly and laughed. He'd gotten really hard and feared he might even shoot off before getting it in, which probably was the drug, since he'd never had that problem before. She'd grabbed his dick and guided it in like she couldn't wait either, and it had seemed great, but despite the way it had felt before, he couldn't seem to come when he was actually fucking her. She was thrashing so much it was like riding a bucking bronco, he'd thought, not that he'd ever had that experience.

He didn't think he'd even been choking her. He'd just put his hands around her throat to try and hold her in place a little. He was shocked when the gout of blood or bloody flesh or whatever it was came out of her mouth, slid down his hand and off to the side. He'd thrown himself back, tried to see what had happened, but it was dark, suddenly much darker than before, as though the moon had disappeared. He'd spoken to her, yelled even, "are you awright" or whatever he'd said, but there was no answer. He'd stumbled to his feet, called for Shannon and Dewey. No response to that either and too dark in the woods to see. He tried to run but kept banging into trees or tripping on underbrush. Finally the moon reappeared, larger than before, and he stumbled back into an open expanse. Shannon and Dewey were there, staring at him, surprised. "Was she with you?" said Shannon.

"She was, but she got sick, and I went looking for you guys."

"Where is she now? She was right here."

"I don't know. She was . . . she threw up some blood or something."

"Look, her clothes are still here," said Dewey. "Is she running around naked somewhere?"

This struck Shannon as funny. "What a weird chick."

"No, she was sick. She was unconscious, I think."

"It's fucking Tales' fault. If I ever catch that little jerkoff again . . ."

They'd looked around for some time, but she was gone. Shannon got bored of it and started insisting she'd probably gone out to the road and caught a ride hitchhiking. "Naked?" Dewey had said. "Sure. I'd pick her up, wouldn't you?" Shannon ever after insisted on the hitchhiking idea, except when he'd get tired of hearing about it and instead say a UFO may have landed while they were running around and aliens abducted her. Dewey stayed quiet. Todd thought something bad had happened, but didn't know what. Maybe something that was his fault. That was why he'd never wanted to try the drug again, even after he scaled down the Bald Cat in the recipe.

Sighing, he opened the *Plan 666* book again, at random.

The A.O.A. retained its widespread reputation as a devil-worshipping cult, while its spinoff, known as The Kindred, was seen by many, especially those with giddily enraptured conceptions of the counterculture in those pre-Manson days of the 1960s, as a proudly warm-and-fuzzy phenomenon of the Aquarian Age. Even so, some of the most bizarre and ultimately murderous tendencies of the A.O.A. were practiced as well by their love-bombing cohorts, who'd themselves germinated in Haight-Ashbury in late 1966. The love-bombing practice itself is most famously associated with the group and, as noted elsewhere, was largely a fund-raising scheme that amounted to little more than ill-disguised prostitution. But according to some, there were Kindred factions that engaged in the truly horrifying "De-braining ritual," a symbolic act of separating the mind from the body, in which corpses were—

His reading was interrupted by a piercing scream from the bathroom, followed quickly by another. He leaped up, tripped over his own feet and hit the floor hard, but scrambled up and ran down the hallway. He found Sky standing naked and dripping wet outside the bathroom, shivering from fear, cold or both, breasts bouncing, dark red public hair. She embraced him as he reached her, the sensual feel and aroma of soaking-wet girl nearly overwhelming him.

"There was some guy looking through the window at me. I just, I freaked out." He let her go, hurried into the bathroom and looked out the window. Nobody was there. Fucking Jaime Tales, who else. He'd been caught looking in people's windows before, and he'd suspected the little retard had been spying on him since Clare had departed.

Sky still stood in the hallway, naked, hands crossed on forearms, shivering.

"I bet I know who it was," he said.

"A friend of yours?"

"No. Little guy with dark hair, beady eyes and no chin?"

She nodded. "Uh-huh, that's him. Let me look for him outside, he might still be around, but he usually runs."

"Is he dangerous?"

"Just a big pussy, is all." He was immediately sorry at the word he'd chosen. "I mean, wuss. You probably scared him away but good."

She tittered. "I scared him, God! I'm still shaking." She hugged Todd again, squirming against him. Put her mouth to his ear, whispered, "I'm so glad you're here with me." Then, oh man, lightly twirling her tongue in there.

Todd was scared himself, and not of Jaime Tales.

15

RONI GOES TO WORK

Roni groused about the encounter with Shannon as she was tolerating the long and bumpy ride on the bus to work. She actually only took the bus because she saw one coming just as she passed the bus stop. It wasn't that far, but she was beat. The bus route took her all over hell and creation before winding up at her destination, which wasn't really very far away. She watched the familiar buildings as the bus went past them. Mad at herself for putting up with the whole place, the whole shebang.

She was still fuming when the bus pulled into the parking lot. Now she'd get to deal with crazy control-freak Hobie and, very likely, his whiny little faggot boyfriend, who'd try to collar her to talk some more. She'd be too busy to bother with him and would tell him so.

Once she got off the bus near the theater, she saw a couple of media trucks with satellite dishes atop them in the parking lot, guys with cameras walking around, and a dolled-up woman reporter with a microphone, apparently interviewing a couple of people, one of whom held a protest sign that read "Satan is Not Lord, But

Deceiver!" This, she knew, was about those "Satan Is Lord" posters Hobie came up with. Naturally, local Bible-thumpers were going to be outraged about it, which was just what he wanted. He'd already been crowing about what a great idea it was, that and all his other stuff, the scarecrows and all, even though all that was probably not going to help attendance at the show.

But something else was going on as well. A small crowd was assembled before an outside wall of the theater. It was the wall Todd Dewolf, the so-called artist, was supposed to be painting a mural on, but the only part of it he'd finished was a little picture of a silver flying saucer up in the upper left-hand corner. However, now something else was there, below that. It was pretty fuzzy and crude but appeared to be an image of a person with their two arms upraised and stretched out. There wasn't much of a face, just a jagged line that could indicate eyes. One arm was bigger than the other, and the smaller one seemed to have not only a hand but what might be a couple fingers. The person didn't have any legs, but there were lines going down either side from where the armpits might be, so it looked like the person could be wearing a kind of gown. *Did Hobie get that put up since last night?* She really doubted Todd came out and did it, though it was so crummy it looked like someone could do it pretty fast. From what Shannon told her, all he did since Clare left him was sit around and drink.

There were more protestors in front of the entrance. One carried a sign that said "The Lord is Not Mocked," and another's said "Satan Walks Among Us." *"Satan Walks Among Us," that sounded like one of Hobie's movie titles.*

Outside the main entrance was a line of four scarecrow-like dummies with hoods over their heads and arms tied behind their backs, being hanged. It looked like the old photos of the outdoor gallows Abraham Lincoln's assassination conspirators were executed from. Hobie had done it himself and was real proud of it. She thought it was hideous and sick, but then, the whole marathon was. But that stuff had also been there yesterday, unlike the mural.

She went into the side entrance, apparently unnoticed by the reporters and the crowd. Once inside, she could hear something scraping across the floor in the next section, the foyer of the theater. Stepping over, she saw Hobie, in striped pajamas, doggedly dragging what looked like a water cooler across the floor. The cooler was full of not water, but some pinkish liquid, and it looked like something else was floating in it. Getting closer, she saw it was a babydoll head.

"Hobie, what in the fuck are you doing now?"

He turned. "Oh, there you are at last! Good morning! I'm just elaborating the Chamber of Horrors theme," he said, grinning. "I've been up all night working on it. Could you go up to my office and fix some coffee? I am totally dead."

"What are you doing with those things?"

"Oh, just setting them up. It's all part of the backdrop. The mise-en-scène, you could say. I've been planning it for some time. It's going to be quite a production, as you'll see."

Mise-en-scène. Christ, he wants to pretend he's making a movie, thought Roni. *With no cameras, yet. What a pathetic wanker.* But Shannon and all his friends were like that, one way or another.

16

JAIME AT THE DONUT HOLE

At the Donut Hole, a tiny donut and coffee restaurant he frequented, Jaime sat before his cup of coffee, stirring in his fourth packet of sugar with a plastic spoon, the emptied sugar packets all scattered on the counter before him, ignoring the scowl from the waitress as she served him his apple fritter on a chipped plate. The fritters they offered were big and cheap.

The TV was going, but Jaime usually didn't pay too much attention and might not have noticed what was being reported at all if a couple of other customers, a trio of old codgers who spoke in the kind of loud voices common to people who can't hear well themselves, hadn't started talking about it in a way that caught his attention.

"Another one? When did this happen?"

"This one was from last year. Chinese girl."

"Looks like she had red hair. That's not normal for them."

"That shows that she's some wild-ass so-and-so type of girl, anyway. Them Chinese people, they usually don't go for that kind of

95

thing."

"She ain't Chinese anyway, she's Korean. I heard her parents got money."

Jaime looked up at the TV, eyes wide, pasty sugar sliding down his chin from his open mouth. *Chinese? Red hair?* His hands began to tremble.

On the TV screen were two photos placed side by side. One that might have come from a high-school yearbook, showing a smiling and pretty girl, her hair black and short. A photo beside it was clearly from later. In it, she was scowling at the camera, had some kind of chain pinned to the side of her lip, and her hair was bright red. A woman reporter was speaking:

"Ms. Cha was last seen on November 20th at the Trocadero Restaurant in the Bennington District. Accounts from witnesses conflict, but some say she was seen leaving the club with a tall slender man with long dark hair and tattoos . . ."

"Where'd they find her?"

"They ain't found her yet. Her parents think she might have been the first victim."

The first victim. That meant Todd Dewolf was the Westside Slasher! He gulped his coffee, burning his mouth, and hurried out.

17

DEWEY AND SHANNON AT THE LIMBO

Dewey was at the Limbo, waiting for Shannon to show up, sitting by the window. He was about an hour late, and Dewey was irritated but not surprised. It still pissed him off about that girl yesterday. It wasn't that he wanted to take her himself. He didn't think that would be safe and didn't have a place to put her anyway, with his grandma around.

It wasn't that the incident with the Asian girl in the woods bothered him that much, though he didn't really have an explanation for what had happened to her. They surely would have heard if she'd been found dead anywhere near there, so somebody probably did pick her up. Maybe she hadn't been totally naked, like, she might have had some other little bathing suit or something in her purse that she got out and put on. Or whatever. It still bugged him Shannon would give this new girl to Todd just because he's such a mess these days. To Dewey, Todd had been messed up even before the thing with the Asian chick. He'd sat in the car when Todd took her inside, and she hadn't said goodbye or looked at him when she left, so he supposed

97

she didn't like him anyway. But there'd never been that many girls who did.

Then there was this whole thing about getting Todd to make worm and dealing it. He was sorry now he'd ever mentioned that magazine article about it to Shannon.

Dewey was drinking his third beer and thinking this was the last one. There were only a few customers around, two guys playing Ms. Pac-Man. Heather wasn't in yet, and Fred had that damned Dr. Landfrey on again. Dewey usually tuned this kind of thing out, but this particular talk caught his attention.

". . . because, friends, the gravest danger, among all the grave dangers, that our country faces today is the homosexual agenda. For you see, homosexuality is not inborn, but is spread by recruitment. It is a thing that a normal person finds loathsome and disgusting, until the key is turned to unlock the sinfulness within. It is a matter of inversion, of going inward, into oneself all alone, which is why self-abuse, according to those who study the workings of the mind, itself leads to homosexuality. As the great Rev. Jonathan Edwards said in 1742, '. . . there is laid in the very nature of carnal man a foundation for the torments of Hell.' And indeed, it is in man that the sin of homosexuality is most foul. For y'see, there is a part of man which, woken up, will become his master. It is a thing laid up deep inside the most intimate part of any normal man, that when abused, becomes like the reproductive parts of a woman. Left alone, it is fine. But once it has been stimulated, and stimulated repeatedly, it will demand more and more unnatural stimulation. It will literally become like a shrewish woman, nagging and whining until it becomes the master to the man, remolding his entire personality into a twisted abomination that amplifies all the worst qualities of woman. And in keeping, there is a part of woman, a tiny thing, that is in some sense like the reproductive part of man, that if awoken . . ."

Dewey wasn't religious and thought this guy was a nut, but this particular sermon troubled him. He feared it might be true, minus the part about religion and sin.

He'd never told anyone about that hitchhiker and never would. It was on a night when he was driving around alone, not real long after Shannon had gotten married and was spending a lot of time at home. He'd been drinking at a bar supposed to be a place to pick up girls, but he didn't know anybody there and nobody came up to talk to him or anything. If they had, he probably wouldn't have handled it well anyway. So he'd sat by himself and got kind of loaded and was on his way home when he saw this girl, short and slender and not bad-looking, it seemed at the time, in jeans and a halter top at the side of the road with her thumb out. *Why not*, he'd thought. She got in right away, was real friendly and talkative, though now he couldn't remember too well what she was talking about, school and her parents being a big drag.

Her name, she'd said, was Chelsea. She had kind of a spiky honey-blonde punk hairdo, wore a lot of makeup and a black choker ribbon around her neck, and had long pendant earrings. Her voice was a little husky like she had a cold. Before long she'd said something about having to pull down her pants and pull up her pantyhose, and somehow from there—how drunk had he been?—they ended up parked behind a closed-down strip mall and together in the back seat.

There wasn't really enough room, the seats weren't designed for stretching out. It was pretty awkward getting clothes off and all, and he was surprised when she rolled over, like she wanted to do it doggy style, and directed his dick up to what he knew right away, despite his limited experience, was not her vagina. It was really tight and did this milking thing that felt great, made him cum in ecstasy. But just after that, he realized there was no other opening and Chelsea wasn't really a girl. He didn't get mad but must have acted appalled because she, or rather he, had acted wary of him and said, "I can walk from here," and he didn't object or say goodbye. He could see him walk off under the street lights and thought he didn't really look that much like a real girl after all.

After that, Dewey was scared he might have gotten AIDS but didn't want to go to the doctor about it. He figured he would have gotten sick by now if he had. There was also some cum smeared on the seat where Chelesa had been lying face down, which he cleaned up real carefully like it was plutonium or something. He worried maybe Hobie Lautenschlager would be able to tell, since he'd heard homos had "gaydar" and could perceive stuff like that. Hobie might even know Chelsea, seemed like they all knew each other. He particularly feared Shannon finding out. Not that Dewey thought he himself was gay, he'd never been interested in guys, but what really bothered him was he'd gotten off better that time than ever before. And there hadn't really been a time since, though he lied about it to Shannon. In jerking off, he stuck to pictures of girls in skin mags, but after Chelsea he almost always fantasized about anal sex.

Following these thoughts, Dewey ordered a fourth beer. The guys playing Ms. Pac-Man had left and another old buzzard had come in, tried to get into a conversation with Fred, but Fred brushed him off with "Yep" and "Nope" and kept watching Dr. TL until the guy gave up. Before he'd finished half of his beer, he saw Shannon's car pull into the parking lot. Finally.

Shannon came in, sat down at the table with Dewey. "Yo," he said, picking up the bottle of beer Dewey had emptied into his glass, and looking it over. "Yeah, I need to get me one of these. Where's Heather?"

"Not here."

"I wonder who's boning her right now," said Shannon as he got up and went to the bar.

Dewey thought about how maybe he ought to pursue Heather himself. His only hesitation was that Shannon would make fun of him over it. He'd never hear the end of it, in fact. Should have asked Shannon to get him another one.

When Shannon came back, turned out he'd gotten Dewey another. "Well, I met those kids and sold 'em the shit," he said.

"Were they mad?"

"Yeah, but fuck it. They got over it. Nice to get a little loot."

"Do you owe Todd now?"

"Yeah, he'll get it." At that point, Jaime Tales came in, glanced at Shannon warily and hurried past him to the bar. "I think I better talk to this asshole," said Shannon. "Or should I?"

"No," said Dewey. "I wouldn't bother."

"Yeah, you're probably right. Well, Roni is pissed, so I don't feel like going home. You wanna play some Ms. Pac?"

"Seriously?"

"Yeah. It's something to do."

They went over to the machine and began to play. Shannon dug into his pocket to get some change, pulling out his car keys and putting them on the machine. After they'd played a few desultory rounds, Dewey really had to piss, and headed for the restroom. "Same here," said Shannon.

They went to the men's room, and one took the toilet and the other the single urinal. "I swear, I love beer but one thing I hate about it is the way it makes your piss smell," said Shannon. They zipped up. Dewey washed his hands and followed Shannon out.

Back at the Ms. Pac-Man machine, Shannon said, "Damn, didn't

I leave some change on this machine?"

"You left your keys there too."

"My fucking keys! Where are they?" He went through his pockets. Dewey looked out the window. "Man, where's your fucking car?"

Shannon looked at the bar, as did Dewey. No Jaime. "You gotta be shittin' me!" yelled Shannon, as Fred and the geezer turned from the TV to look at him in alarm.

18

TODD, HAVING FAILED

Sky lay back, smoking a cigarette, and Todd sat up on the edge of the bed, feeling more awkward than he had in many years, maybe since puberty in junior high. He might even have wept, had he been alone, but stifled it hard.

"I'm sorry. I'm just a little nervous, I guess. It's like, my wife left and, you know, it's been a long time."

She put her hand on his, squeezed. She smiled dazzlingly. "Hey, it's no problem. It happens."

He forced a laugh. "It's embarrassing." There was no way to be cool about this.

"Don't be, it's fine. I like just making out sometimes." Her voice was soft and breathy. She rolled over and sat beside him, put a leg between his, grasped his shoulders and turned him toward her in an embrace, pushed him back onto the bed, squirming over him, herself on top. She made pecking kisses all over his face, tongued his ear, rubbed the top of his head and set her hand gently on the side of his face, as a mother might do to console an unhappy toddler. Face

105

to his, she studied him for a moment, pouted cutely as if to say he still looked sad, put her arms around his neck and kissed him hard on the mouth, nibbling at his lips, pushing her tongue into his mouth and friskily twisting it around. He submitted to it all, like she was the guy and he was the girl.

She reached into his open pants, fished around for his dick, gave a soft squeeze. He felt some stirring there, but not enough, not nearly enough. She withdrew her hand quickly. God, how humiliating was this going to be?

"Sorry," he mumbled.

"It's okay."

"You're awfully understanding." He sounded a bit sarcastic, without meaning to.

"Sure, why not? After all, I love you."

He wasn't sure she'd said what he thought she'd said. "You do what?"

"I love you." She gave him a brief, emphatic kiss on the lips.

"Do you love everybody? This isn't, like, a hippie thing? Peace and love and all that?"

She laughed. "I like that old-fashioned love thing. But I mean you. I love you. You, you, you!"

She tickled him on his sides under his arms, like an adult teasing a child. He struggled not to laugh.

"Thanks," he said. "I mean," and it was hard to speak the words, "I love you, too." At that, she leaned close to his face again, grinning, put her hands at the top of his head and roughed up his hair.

"Would you like some wine?" said Todd, flat on his back in the bed. He sure would.

"Yeah, that'd be great," she said. "Could we get something to eat, too?" Nude, she jumped up, knelt to pick up his bathrobe from the floor, wrapped it around herself and tied the belt.

"Oh, I'm sorry, are you hungry?" *Stupid question.*

"Kind of," she said. "Are you?"

"I could eat something," he said, but what he really wanted to do was drink. Eating would interfere with his buzz. "I need to go to the store, but I think I have some salami and cheese. Don't have any bread right now, though. Got some cans of soup."

"We could just have wine for now," she said.

"Great, I'll get some." He went into the kitchen, got glasses out of the cabinet, rinsed them out since they'd been unused forever. He checked out his stash of wine. Damn, there wasn't much, he'd have to go to the store to get more. He didn't like to think they could smell it on his breath.

Sky called from the other room. "Hey, can I look through your movies?"

"Sure, go ahead," he said. *Uh-oh. Will she be disgusted they're all porn?*

He heard the sound of music and voices; she must have turned on the TV. He stepped back into the room and saw she'd put in a video. It was one he probably hadn't rewound, since he wasn't good about doing that. Looked like it was one of the *Latex Dreams* series, with the toothy girl who always went "Hrnt! Hrnt!" when she was having sex.

"So where'd you get all these movies?"

"Well, see, I used to run a video store, Exquisite Corpse, along with this guy named Hobie Lautenschlager, who I knew from school."

"I never heard of that. Exquisite Corpse?"

"It wasn't part of a chain. We just had the one shop. We mostly had horror movies, but we also got porn because, you know, it's popular. Hobie had some money to invest in it, so it was pretty much his shop, really, though we were supposed to be partners.

"Hobie's kind of a weird guy. He's interested in the occult and voodoo and stuff. He's interested in some Jamaican writer named Alberic Crabtree."

"Yeah, I've heard of him."

"Oh." Todd wasn't sure this was a good thing. "Are you, like, a fan or anything?"

"No." She seemed fairly adamant about it, but said no more.

"Okay. Me neither. How about Paradise Threshold, ever hear of that?"

She seemed a bit uncomfortable, hearing this. "Yeah, they were out there in Manhattan Beach. They were strictly ufology. They're all dead."

Todd was going to ask where Manhattan Beach was, but instead said, "Dead?"

"They committed suicide because they thought they were going to soul-travel off and merge with a comet."

"Did that have to do with this Crabtree guy?"

"I don't know, maybe somehow."

Hmmm. "Well anyway, Hobie was all into that guy's work, and he

107

related it all to horror movies, which he also was crazy about. We had trouble at the shop because Hobie would do these weird things, like, somewhere he found a human skeleton, a real dirty one, like it had been dug up out of the ground—"

"Yikes, really?"

"Yeah, and he took it and stuffed it into an old TV with a smashed screen so it looked like it was coming out of the TV and put that in the shop's front window. Which would have been kind of an appropriate thing for a video store that mostly had horror movies, but it was a real skeleton, so I was afraid the cops or the health department at least would hassle us about it. I had a real hard time talking him out of having that in the window. I mean, otherwise, he did a good job of managing the shop.

"Then he got all interested in this old soft drink they used to sell in voodoo shops in New Orleans a long time ago. He thought it had all these kind of magical properties, and all this." He decided he wasn't going to tell her about how you made the drug worm from it, and that he'd been cooking up some himself lately because the guy who'd brought her over asked him to. It seemed too complicated, and she might not like it that he cooked up dope.

"So, after a while, Hobie lost interest in the shop because he had a chance to rent this old dilapidated movie theater in town. He's been running that for a few months. It was like his dream to run a movie theater and show horror movies. I was supposed to be in on it, but bailed out. I think he's going to burn up all his money on it."

"So you worked there, too?"

"Not really. All I ever did was try to paint a mural on an outside wall, but I never finished it." Barely started it, in fact, but he didn't say that.

"You're an artist, huh?"

"Oh. Well, yeah. I went to art school for a while. Dropped out."

"I bet you're real talented. You seem like an artist."

"No, I've kind of given it up."

"Aw, that's a drag. You just need more self-confidence." The girl on the TV screen went on making her signature sound. Sky turned her head and looked down at him, smiling happily. "So is this guy's name 'Hrnt'?"

He forced a laugh. "No, that's just a sound she makes."

"Really, why do you like these movies so much?"

Todd didn't like to get defensive about it, but it was hard not to.

"I don't exactly like them, I don't think."

"What do you watch them for?"

He wondered if she was asking him about jerking off. He'd feel silly denying it, so didn't bother.

"I'm kind of trying to figure something out about them. Like, why they're so depressing after a while. I know that sounds goofy."

"Omigod!" She put her hand on his. "I know what you mean! You have to stay engaged with it or it gets really awful."

She ran her hand down his upper arm. "I like that tattoo on your arm. Where'd you ever get that?"

"Oh," he said, glancing at it, holding it out so she could look at it more closely. "At a tattoo parlor."

She stroked her fingers over the image. "She's beautiful."

"Thanks."

"That's not her, is it? Your wife?"

"No." He didn't want to explain, it wouldn't have made sense.

Sky turned back to the TV. The nude girl on the screen rolled over onto her knees, and the guy, middle-aged, fat and wearing only black socks, repositioned behind her and visibly inserted, pumping and groaning unpleasantly as she continued with, "Hrnt!" Sky pulled up her legs, letting the robe fall open, and put her hand at her crotch. Todd couldn't see what she was doing from his angle, but apparently she was, omigod, playing with herself. She just wasn't going to let up. She started imitating the cry of the girl in the movie. "Hrnt! Hrnt!"

The scene seemed to go on for a long time, though Todd looked only at Sky and not again at the TV. He could smell the distinct odor of fresh female wetness emanating from Sky. She stopped making the "Hrnt" sound, was breathing harder and faster, finally gasped, leaning her head on her knees and pulling her legs up tighter.

Well, it was what she needed after all that build-up, he supposed. The scene in the porn video was still going on, as he could hear. He thought about the littleness of his dick, compared to porn actors anyway, about his lack of stir in the bedroom, and found he couldn't move at all. She pulled her hand up, licked her fingers and palm and wiped them off on the hem of the robe.

"You know what?" she said. "You got some scary shit around here."

"What do you mean?" He still didn't think he could move.

"Duh! Like that bedpost with big nails driven into it?"

"Oh, that." It was an old wooden bedpost with several very large nails driven into it at the top, pitched at different directions, leaning against the wall near the front door. "Someone made it because they were having a problem with a neighbor a few years ago. I kind of inherited it." In fact, Shannon had come up with the thing years back when he was having a bitter conflict with Bud Junior, one of the older Tales brothers, over a parking space near both their houses.

"What about that axe?" She pointed at the large ax in a decorative stand by the fireplace.

"That's for chopping wood for the fireplace. I never do, it's just a decoration now."

He wasn't going to tell her about the other dangerous items he owned—his collection of switchblades and ninja throwing stars or the sawed-off 12-gauge shotgun he traded his old Danelectro bass for when he gave up on music. He liked to collect stuff like that. Old cars, too, but he didn't have any cars anymore except the Thunderbird, which Shannon was using.

"Okay. Well, I guess that's cool then."

"Hmmm. Well, we need more wine, so I'm going to the store," he said. "Would you like me to get something else? Something to eat later?"

"Do they have salads?"

"Like, prepared salads? Yeah, I guess they do." They used to, because Clare used to get them.

"That'd be great," she said. "Oh, and Todd? Some oysters." She made a somewhat wicked face.

He paused. Oysters. "Okay."

"Do you like oysters?"

"Not sure I've had them."

"Get two or three tins of them, if you would."

"Sure." *Hmm.*

He put on his coat, headed for the door. "Hurry back," she said, looking over her shoulder and smiling with her full face. Those strange, intense eyes.

19

JAIME IN TODD'S CAR

Jaime was a little surprised at how hard to steer the big car was. He'd only driven two cars before, both of them pretty little, though he didn't know what kind they were. One was light blue and the other kind of dark red, except for one door which was white with dribbled brown stains on it. He told himself he knew all about driving, was really good at it, but just didn't get a chance to do it that much. His brother Marlon had sneered at him and said he couldn't drive at all 'cause he was stupid and chickenshit, but Marlon was always saying putdowns, to him and to everybody. But especially to him. But if Marlon could see him now, he'd be impressed, even if he wouldn't admit it.

He kept thinking about what to say to Clare when he saw her, trying to compose his sentences beforehand so he didn't mess up. The reason he was doing this was because she'd asked him to before she'd left Stankerton. It was one night at the Limbo when she and Veronica were there together. They both seemed to be upset and were talking in hushed but emotional voices. Veronica kept saying something like "I don't blame you, but Clare, seriously, this other stuff isn't real," and Clare kept going on and on, sounding mad but saying stuff he couldn't make out, though Veronica seemed to want to break in and kept shaking her head no. Finally, Veronica got up and left, said, "Okay, call me though. Okay? Clare?" But Clare didn't say anything. After Clare left, Heather went over and tried to talk to Clare, but Clare must have said something nasty, because Heather said, "Fine," like she was offended, and walked back into the kitchen.

That left Clare and Jaime alone in the Limbo for a minute. He was still watching her, and she looked up at him, grabbed her purse and came over, like she was mad at him, which alarmed him. She put her hands on the table he sat at, leaned into his face and said, in a real angry voice, "If you want to watch people, watch Todd Dewolf. Watch him and let me know when *she* shows up."

"Okay," he'd said meekly, though he wasn't sure who she meant. *Veronica?*

"I'll be down at Aunt Beulah's in Dayville. My real aunt, your uncle's widow. Come and tell me when she does. *Cousin.*" She said the word like she was spitting it out, turned and left.

So he wasn't really "telling," like a tattletale, that his brothers used to wail on him about, and that his mom even smacked him for once when she didn't want to hear what he was telling her about how he'd seen Cheryl Sue and that woman she worked with at the old folks home kissing on each other in that car with the white door. He only told because he was baffled over why they'd be doing that, since they were both girls. Both ugly, too.

So that was one of the only reasons he had to take Todd's car from Shannon and drive down to Dayville, and the other only reason was that Todd might be the Westside Slasher if that China girl was one of his victims like they said on TV. He had to be careful, though, not to say too much about what happened after what he saw Shannon and Todd do in the woods.

But how did Clare know this girl was going to come and stay with Todd? She must have known her before. It all didn't make sense.

He had to take the car, and it seemed like he was somehow supposed to, when he saw those keys on the Ms. Pac-Man machine just when he was thinking about how in the world he was going to get to Dayville to call Clare. But now he was more and more worried the cops might be after him, especially since he'd been driving around for longer than it should have taken to get there because he thought maybe he was lost.

Jaime had been nervous through most of the trip, driving down the highway past endless sweeps of forestland and farms that seemed to go on forever. He thought he knew what highway to take from back when they used to go see Maamaw in Dayville, and sometimes Aunt Beulah, though they didn't always get along with her, and Maamaw didn't like her at all, though they were half-sisters, Beulah being a lot younger. It was the one with the exit sign that said "New Ashville 25 miles." It used to be on the one he thought he was on, because it was right past where the old Wink-O Lanes bowling place was, and he had seen that building, but now everything was different. *Could that be the wrong side of the building?*

But before long, to his great relief, he saw the milestone he'd remembered, a life-size cow on a high post advertising a dairy and restaurant. He'd never seen those places because when you saw the cow you looked for the exit to Dubert Avenue off the highway. That took you pretty quick to a big cemetery, and on the other side of the street was first a strip mall, which, yep, there it was, though it looked like it was all closed now, and then a large and very rundown trailer park. A couple blocks past that were some houses, spread far apart. Aunt Beulah's house, he remembered, was green and the house number 1616 was painted on the mailbox by the road in big black letters.

As he approached it, he saw the house was faded to a kind of green-gray, the paint was chipping off, the lawn was overgrown in places and gouged out elsewhere, but the mailbox still bore those numbers. He made it! He did pretty good time, too. He was pleased he'd managed this—see, he could drive real good. But now he had to go knock on the door and talk to somebody.

He went up to the door and was astonished when his Maamaw answered it. How could it be? She was dead! And she scowled at him angrily, which wasn't like her, even after she got sick.

"What you want?"

"I'm lookin' for Beulah Tales."

"Ain't been Beulah Tales for years. What you want?" She had bourbon on her breath. His mother drank it all the time too. He did sometimes, but more than a little made him sick.

"I'm just, I'm just lookin' for Aunt Beulah, Beulah Hardwick Tales, I mean, Beulah Tales Hardwick, 'cause she's my grandma's sister. And I'm lookin' for Clare. Clare Hardwick. 'Cause she lives here."

"Not for long," she said, "not for long." She squinted. "Good

Lord, you're that goddamned Bud Tales Junior."

"Naw, I'm Jaime."

"You ain't Bud and Sally's boy?"

"That's my ma, Sally Tales, but I'm Jaime." She was Aunt Beulah, she just looked different. A lot older. She didn't look like Maamaw before.

"Jaime Tales? The little one that's stupid?" He didn't answer, just stared. "What the hell you people want now?" she went on. "You done took Pa for everything he had, long ago." She was swaying.

"I'm lookin' for Clare Hardwick."

"You want Clare? Good. Come on in and fuckin' take her." His grandmother would never have said "fuckin'." The room was well-kept but the house smelled of Lysol and some kind of decay beneath that. The TV was on, but the sound was off.

"*Clare!*" screamed Aunt Beulah. "Getchur ass down here, ya damn baby stealin' whore!"

She turned to Jaime. "You know what she done? Was working at the Hardwick Funeral Home, which we don't run no more since Pa Hardwick sold it, and a goddamn dead baby turned up missing. A dead baby! After they talked to her, it turned up again outside the funeral home, on the steps the next morning, all decayed." She pointed upstairs. "But I could *smell* it afterward when I went up there. You could *smell* it had been in that little whore's room! She's crazier than your father and my husband and the whole bunch of them! Calls herself a Hardwick!"

Someone was at the top of the stairs, stepping down. It was Clare, wearing a lightweight yellow dress and worn, dingy tennis shoes. She was much thinner than when he'd last seen her, looked starved even, and her hair looked like something had gnawed it off close to her skull.

Aunt Beulah scowled at her as she descended. "Did you know the Tales boy was comin' to getcha? You probably did. You know everything, your highness."

Clare didn't speak, came calmly to the bottom of the stairs, glanced briefly at Jaime but didn't look surprised to see him. She didn't acknowledge Beulah at all. "Queen Shit," said Beulah, but Clare didn't seem to hear.

"Too good to even look for work. Nobody'd hire her anyway, after she took that baby."

Clare sat down on a sofa near where Jaime stood. Suddenly she screamed, "*Will you shut up?!*"

"I'll shut up when you—"

Clare picked up a sofa pillow and threw it at Beulah. "*Get out!*"

Beulah retreated into the kitchen, saying "Call the damn police, that's what I'll do."

Clare looked at Jaime, said "Yes?"

Jaime found he was out of breath. "I come to tell you."

"Tell me what?"

"What you said. About Todd."

Clare gazed out the front window. "You have Todd's car. The Thunderbird."

"Yeah."

"Did Todd send you here?"

"No, he's back in Stankerton. I mean, no, he didn't."

"I don't understand."

"You said to tell you that a girl came. A girl. You said to tell you. At the Limbo." He was flustered, sounded to himself like a tattletale.

She sat quietly, running her fingers through her hair, acting troubled. They could hear Aunt Beulah talking on the phone in another room, past the kitchen, yelling incoherently.

"Okay, let's go," said Clare. She went back up the stairs. Some minutes passed, and finally Jaime sat on the sofa himself, watching the silent TV. It showed that preacher guy Fred at the Limbo had on all the time

Beulah came back into the room, said, "Where's she?"

"Upstairs," he said.

"You leaving?"

"I guess . . ."

"Well, take her with you, 'cause she sure as shit ain't staying—"

Clare came down the stairs again, carrying a big plaid suitcase that seemed to be heavy.

"You're really leavin', finally!" said Beulah. She smiled at Jaime. "Are you ever in for it."

"Let's go," said Clare, opening the front door.

"Don't come back, neither one of yas," said Beulah, her voice breaking. "Hardwicks, my fuckin' ass."

20

SHANNON AND DEWEY AT THE TALES' HOME

After some discussion in which Dewey had advocated, reasonably he thought, that they should tell Todd about his car being stolen, a move Shannon rejected with annoyance, they were driving along in silence for a while. Without saying anything, Shannon pulled into somebody's driveway, backed out, and drove off back in the direction they'd just come.

"Where are we going now?" asked Dewey.

"I'm gonna see if fuckin' retard Jaime is home, or if the other retards know where he is," said Shannon.

"You mean, at the Tales' house over on Dodsworth?"

"Yes."

"I don't think he lives there anymore."

"Yeah. Well, if he doesn't, maybe someone there will be conscious enough to tell me where he does live. Okay?"

"Sure. Whatever you want. Just don't go in there and call them retards or hilljacks or something. You know, they get pretty serious about shit."

"Yes, I know," said Shannon. "I'm fucking familiar with them."

They drove on. Dewey thought about the time years ago when he saw Jaime and some other Tales outside the entrance to the A&P grocery store at a strip mall, his mom standing around talking to some other woman in a loud, cawing voice. Jaime kept interrupting, begging for a quarter so he could get something he wanted in a gumball machine. Mrs. Tales got enraged and hollered, "Lick my worm, boy!" Heads turned, but the woman Mrs. Tales was speaking to didn't react, just went on talking. Jaime had been a kid then, but not that little.

When they arrived at the Tales' house, it looked like it might be unoccupied except for the ancient hound dog sitting in a mudhole at the edge of the front lawn, which was overgrown in the spots where it wasn't bare. As they stepped up to the front door, the dog woofed at them, turned and rose up, and started walking slowly and unsteadily toward them.

"They still have Baby," said Shannon, for that had been their dog's name years before.

"Unless that's his grandson," said Dewey.

The door was open, a TV was going inside, but no one answered when they knocked. Shannon stepped inside, saying, "Yo! Hello?" Dewey sighed and went after him. The dog was at their heels, woofing more and whimpering as he struggled along. Inside, the house smelled like burned microwave popcorn.

The TV was in the living room with the sound up loud, but no one was watching it. "Well, shit," Shannon said. "Hello? Mrs. Tales? Anybody?" The dog followed, wheezing, and managed another woof, this one ending with a weak, sad-sounding howl.

"Baby, what you doin' in the house?" came a voice from a room down the hall, and then a loud sneeze. There was, in fact, the sound of another TV coming from the same direction. They stepped down the hallway and turned into a room, which turned out to be a bathroom, for in it, they saw a very fat naked woman sitting in a bathtub full of sudsy water, watching a small TV perched upon the toilet beside the tub.

Shannon and Dewey ducked back out. Dewey was about to run for the door, but Shannon said "'Scuse me, ma'am, we were lookin' for Jaime?"

After a long moment of silence, the woman said, "Who's that out there?"

"Shannon Boner. I'm a friend of Jaime's."

"Jaime who?"

"Jaime Tales."

She groaned and muttered. "Hold on 'til I get outta the tub."

Dewey felt something bump his ankle and turned to find it was the dog, who apparently was trying to bite him, but lacked the jaw strength to do so, or perhaps the teeth, or both. He woofed again.

"Dammit, Baby, you ain't s'posed to be in this house," said the fat woman as she stepped out of the bathroom in a badly stained, too-small robe that had once been white and a bath towel over her hair. Dewey, avoiding a close look at her blubbery exposed bosoms, belly and thighs, focused on her face, and felt a glimmer of recognition. Could this be Cheryl Sue Tales, whom he'd been in high school with? She was fat back then, but nothing like this. He'd heard about her over the years, but hadn't seen her in all that time.

"Hey, Cheryl, you remember me, right?" said Shannon. "Shannon Boner."

"Yeah, unfortunately I do. Just walk into people's houses, huh?" Baby woofed again, twice, louder, and then whimpered as if frustrated at not getting attention. "It's okay, Baby. Shut up." Cheryl waddled forward into the living room and collapsed onto a red vinyl lounger. "Who you lookin' for? Jaime? He don't live here."

"We thought you might know where he is."

"I ain't seen Jaime in six months. You say you're his friend? When you get to be friends?"

"Well, I've known him a long time and all."

"If you're his friend, how come you don't know where he is?"

"Just don't."

"What you wanna see 'im about?"

"I owe him some money. I want to pay him back."

Cheryl Sue laughed at that, and Shannon joined in, but Cheryl quit laughing and looked mean again after a couple moments. She rubbed her hair with the towel, kicking up an odor of shampoo and sweat.

"Well, I'll tell ya for sure, I don't know where he is an' I don't give a shit. If you find him, tell him his goddamn mother's in the hospital dyin', probably gonna have to go on kidney dialysis."

Frustrated, Baby began barking viciously as Cheryl was speaking, but she ignored him. It sounded convincing, like he was about to rip someone's leg off, but he was wobbling in place as he did so. He nipped weakly at Shannon's calf, enough that Shannon said, "Dog, goddammit," and kicked his leg backward, shoving him aside.

Baby fell over flat on his side, whimpering, hyperventilating and trembling violently, his entire abdomen inflating and deflating like a bagpipe.

"What'd you do?" screamed Cheryl. "You hurt Baby! You kicked him!"

"No, I didn't," said Shannon. "I just moved him with my foot."

"He's havin' a stroke! You sonovabitch!" She jumped up and thumped into the bedroom. They heard a scraping sound from there, and Cheryl emerged with a rifle in hand. Shannon and Dewey took off fast as she fired, once and again, though the blasts came nowhere near them, seemed to go into the ceiling.

They heard something falling to the floor and Cheryl Sue yelling, "Hell, shit!" as they bounded across the lawn, climbed into the Chevy and skidded away.

21

RONI AT THE MIRROR

"The same admission on Saturday as on Friday night?" The kid stared at Roni, trying to be intimidating. He had a large knapsack, one you might take to climb a mountain, and had set it on the floor in front of the ticket booth. She wondered for a moment if he might have a gun in it.

"Yes, that's correct." She was trying to see people's hands as they strode by, looking for those hand stamps.

"I'm sorry, but that doesn't make any sense. Could I speak to someone who knows what they're doing?"

"This is the setup. The manager made it very clear." Roni pointed to the sign. She thought it was stupid and unfair herself, but it wouldn't help to say so.

"I doubt that. Where is the manager?" The guy eyed her oddly. She was pretty sure he was looking at her stain.

"He's not available."

"This is completely ridiculous. The full admission is for eleven movies. Four of those movies have already been shown." People were walking by to the concession stand and the auditorium beyond it, not showing their hand stamps. A lot of them might have paid already and were coming back, but somebody needed to check those as people came in. That was the security guard's job, but the guy they'd hired, Glenn, was not at the table by the inner entrance as he was supposed to be. She'd noticed he was gone at least twenty minutes before.

"I'm sorry you don't like the policy, but I can't change it and the manager won't change it. That's it."

"It really is so unfair," came a familiar voice. Standing beside him was Benny, looking at her as if offended, taking the side of the guy complaining, who ignored him. Didn't look like they knew each other. Benny probably thought he was cute. Benny wore a one-piece, black, form-fitting Danskin outfit—it wasn't supposed to be a costume, he'd aspired to be a professional dancer, never got anywhere but never got over it, Hobie had said—and had a new hairstyle, a kind of jheri-curl. It looked ridiculous.

"Why isn't the manager here?" said the knapsack guy.

"Because," sighed Roni, "he isn't here."

"It'll be a cold day in hell when I come back to this theater." He picked up his heavy knapsack and put it on his back.

"I, for one, don't blame you," said Benny as the guy walked off without responding.

Benny came forward and leaned on the ledge of the ticket booth. "You were just saying that, weren't you? About Hobie?" He too seemed to be looking right at the side of her eye.

"Thanks a lot for making my job easier."

"I'm—what? Are you being sarcastic?" He seemed surprised. "I felt the situation called for someone to show a little sympathy for what he was saying. You noticed, I'm sure, he calmed down as soon as I spoke. You know, you catch more flies with honey than with vinegar."

"Thanks, I'll try to remember that one." She looked over at the people standing in long lines to the restrooms, some of them looking quite uncomfortable, like they had to go pretty bad. There was only one toilet in each room, plus a urinal in the men's room. People were still going past the ticket booth, still no Glenn.

"But he is here, isn't he? He wouldn't leave with his marathon going on. He's put his whole heart and soul into it. Is he in his office?"

"No, I was just up there. No." In fact, that was probably where

121

he was. "I don't know where he is, haven't seen him in the last hour. He might be in the projection booth with Larry." Larry was their quiet, very competent projectionist. "Or he may have gone home."

"Please be honest with me. I need to see him one more time, even if from a distance. I don't even want to speak to him. You can understand that, can't you? You've been in a heartbreaking relationship yourself. I want to see him once more, to say my private farewell just to myself. Then I'm going away, forever."

"Well, if you hang around here long enough, you'll probably see him eventually. Right now, you're holding up the line, okay?"

"You know, I didn't want to be the one to tell you about your husband. He's involved in this thing, too. He shares responsibility for what's going on here in the theater, with Hobie and with many, many other people."

"What are you talking about now?" she said, but Benny stalked away.

A couple, guy and girl, came up next. The guy had a cheap Darth Vader mask but wore ordinary clothes, while the girl was done up in an elaborate Princess Leia costume.

"What's the admission for just Saturday?" asked the guy. He sounded cranky, and the girl looked mad. Roni had a feeling they already knew and wanted to bitch.

"It's twenty-seven dollars, the same as for Friday night. Covers admission for Sunday, too."

"What about just for Saturday?"

"Twenty-seven dollars."

"I'm sorry?" he said, raising his voice some, and the girl smirked.

"Twenty-seven dollars is the fee no matter what." She pointed wearily to the sign.

"That's the same as if you come Friday night."

More people moved past. Roni noticed the guy she'd previously been arguing with about the price, with the knapsack, on the far side of them, going inside. She wasn't going to stop him.

She wanted to talk to Hobie herself. She didn't like this thing with the pink water in the water coolers. You wouldn't think anybody would drink that stuff when it had rubber spiders and babydoll heads floating in it, but there were paper cups in a tube attached to the coolers, and she'd already seen two people sipping out of those cups.

22

JAIME AND CLARE

"How much money do you have?" said Clare. They passed Wink-O Lanes, so Jaime was pretty sure he knew which way to go now.

"I don't have none."

"What about money for gas?"

He blanched. Hadn't thought about that. Looking at his face, Clare shook her head, said, "Just drop me off at the bus station."

He looked at the dashboard. Where was the gas? He thought the round dial was it. Looked like the needle was almost straight up.

"We got enough to get to Stankerton."

"Why would I want to go there? I'm going to Los Angeles."

"I thought you were coming with me."

"Why would I do that?"

"You ain't give me a chance to tell you."

"I'm not interested in anything that has to do with Stankerton."

"But you come with me from Aunt Beulah's when I showed up."

"I needed to get out of there. I had my bag packed already."

"But it was like you knew I was coming." He sounded like he was whining, something his brothers and sisters used to smack him around for. Remembering that Clare was his cousin, he raised one shoulder as a bulwark.

"I knew something would happen. It was time for me to go."

"I come to tell you about this girl. She's stayin' there with Todd now."

She spoke more sharply than before. "I don't care what he does anymore."

"But this girl, see, she's not the only one. There was this other one. And she . . . do you get the news down here?"

"What news?"

"About the girls in Stankerton. All the girls that are gettin' killed."

Clare shrugged. "I don't know what you're talking about."

"It's a serial killer, and he's killing these girls. And this one girl, she got killed out in the woods. And right now there's this Halloween thing at the movie theater, and there's all these crowds because of the wall."

"What wall?"

"The wall Todd was going to paint on. There's a picture on there now."

"You mean Todd finished the mural?" Now she sounded interested.

"No, it just got there. It was there this morning. Wasn't there yesterday. And people are going to see it. They think it's a Jesus picture."

"A Jesus picture? An image of Christ?"

"Yeah."

"Where Todd was working on his mural?" She stared at him wide-eyed.

"Yeah. The one with the little flying saucer on it."

"So he finished the mural after all. Interesting. You're sure about this?"

"Sure I'm sure."

"I'm not sure I believe you."

He hated being accused of lying, used to get that from his siblings a lot too. "Why would I say it? Come and see. Plus, Todd, you know, he's—"

"These dead girls, do they say anything about their hearts?"

"Well . . ." *How'd she know that?* "Their hearts, they say they get cut out. Sometimes."

124

Clare seemed very satisfied with this. "Cut out, hah! Those are the Qwiff."

"The what?" A car passing them in the opposite direction honked as Jaime strayed slightly into the adjacent lane.

"Watch where you're driving," said Clare. "The exit is coming up. My my, the Qwiff and the mural. It's all happening just as Delbert Wingdale said it would. And Todd in the middle of it all. I always told him he was fated."

23

TODD AND SKY

When Todd returned from the store, he found Sky still watching TV but not masturbating. She was still in his robe. She turned and smiled winningly.

"Hey, did you get some good stuff?"

"I think so. Wine and oysters. Got you a salad, too. Caesar salad."

"Yummy! Did you get yourself one?"

"I'm not that hungry."

"You like never eat, do you? That's bad for you when you're drinking."

"Yeah, it probably is."

"I'm not trying to scold you or anything. I'm just worried about you, darling." She got up from the rocking chair, came toward him, embraced him. As she did, she grabbed him by one butt cheek. "I told you I love you. And I'm not nearly done with you yet, buster."

Maybe she thought he couldn't fuck because of malnutrition. "I have some stuff to eat, some baloney and potato chips and stuff. I'll have some."

"Oh, that sounds healthy," she laughed.

"Speaking of healthy, you want some wine?"

"Yeah! Let's have some oysters, too," she said brightly. "I gotta go to the bathroom again. Hope nobody looks in the window and watches me pee."

He went into the kitchen, set down the bags. The frying pans he'd cooked up the worm in the night before were still in the sink. Aphrodisiac effect. But what about Lenore? Maybe just a taste. He picked up a pan that had some residue in it, licked it. It was more bitter than he'd remembered and seemed to seethe on his tongue.

24
RONI CONFRONTS HOBIE

Someone knocked at the door to the ticket booth, behind Roni. *What? This wasn't Hobie, was it?*

"Me," someone called from behind it. It was Stella. Roni jumped up, opened it.

"Hey," said Stella. "I'm still sick as a dog, but I decided to come in." She coughed softly twice, hand over mouth. Sounded fake, but she was here, thank God.

"Great. Could you take over the booth right now? I have to go find fucking Glenn. He's not at his desk and people are just walking in for free."

"I know, I saw. Asshole. We should have gotten a rent-a-cop."

Hobie was too penny-foolish for that, but it wasn't worth saying. "I'll be back," said Roni.

Roni couldn't find Glenn anywhere through the hallways, decided to try the auditorium. She stepped inside, just in time to catch the finish of a preview, in which a screaming, decayed corpse/zombie's head exploded, the scattered brain matter adhering to walls of a padded cell, coming alive with tarantulas. The audience whooped with approval. The words "Don't Dare To See It Alone!" appeared on the screen but cut off abruptly and were replaced with an animated cartoon image of a happy-looking goateed beatnik in a striped jersey, sunglasses and beret playing bongo drums. The beatnik, still smiling broadly, pulled out a gun and shot his head completely off so that it disappeared, bringing more whoops. The words "Crazy cool! It's from Bongoville, Daddy-O!" appeared under the stilled image and quickly blipped away.

That scene was replaced by an approaching dolly-shot to a lighted window in a house at night, which moved through the window to show a young and nude male and female couple fornicating very theatrically in bed, both thrashing and breathing hard, a bright flickering lantern on an end table by the bed. The girl spoke in a wavering voice that rose with each beat, ". . . almost, almost, almost, it's, it's, omigod yes, it's—" The scene was replaced by stock footage of a nuclear mushroom cloud, superimposed over which were the flying heads and limbs of apparently the couple seen just previously, followed by the scrolling words:

ARMAGEDDON OUTTA HERE!
Directed by Marty the Martian Martin
A Bongoville Production

There was applause and laughter from the audience.

Roni groaned softly, looking around. As the screen lit up repeatedly with the continuing atomic explosion, she caught a glimpse of Glenn, sitting in the back row, watching the movie and eating popcorn.

She hurried over to his aisle. "Yoo-hoo, Glenn," she said in a low but testy voice. "You're supposed to be at the security desk."

"Oh, hi," he said, looking surprised and downcast. "I was checking things out in here and sat down for a minute."

"Where'd you get the popcorn?"

"Somebody left it here, so I was just having a handful."

"Please go back to the security desk right now. We really need you there."

"All right," he said, getting up and sounding annoyed.

Christ, sorry to interrupt you. Next time we should make sure the guard we hire isn't a dumb-ass movie fan.

As she stepped through the door of the auditorium, two girls came up to her, dressed in identical leopard-skin miniskirts, tall black boots and white sleeveless crop tops made of imitation fur. One had a trim waist and the other was pudgy, so one looked good and the other only managed to emphasize her worst features. Someone should tell her. "Hey, you work here, right?"

"Yes, why?" Roni wanted to get a cigarette before she went back to the ticket booth. This would delay that.

"Are people supposed to drink that pink water in the water coolers?"

"I sure wouldn't. It's got babydoll heads in it and all that." *Really, how could anyone drink that?*

"Because some people are, and it's making them really sick," said the fat girl. She twisted her mouth around, making a grossed-out face.

"I don't know why anybody'd—"

"You can't drink at the water fountain. It's turned off," said the skinny one. Hobie's doing.

Hoo boy.

Roni heard someone nearby moaning and hacking, ending with the unmistakable sound of puke being hurled. Several voices went "Ewwww!" in out-of-key unison, like a chorus of yowling alley cats.

There were more voices: "What's he doing now?" and "I dunno. Look at him. Jesus."

Roni rushed to the place where the voices came from, the leopard-skin girls following after. A boy in fairly standard corpse paint and zombie gear was on all fours on the floor, his face hanging above a pinkish pool of vomit, retching as if trying hard to add to it. A crowd surrounding him watched, mostly appalled, though some were grinning.

"Fuck, I had some too," said a guy in a Tor Johnson mask. "I thought it was just colored water."

"Really, you drank some of that shit?" said another, wearing a KFC bucket as a hat. "Yeech! What did it taste like?"

"Kind of like beets."

"That sounds horrible. Are you going to puke too?"

The one who'd drank belched, covered his mouth. "I dunno yet. Yeah, I think I am."

"Uh-oh. Look out, you guys!" Onlookers backed away from him as he began to make chugging sounds. His eyes were darting around frantically.

The kid on his knees stopped retching, and his limbs slipped out so his turned face went into the puddle of puke.

"Ewwwww!" came the chorus again, more emphatic than before. Another kid, this one with Spock ears, came up to the girls in leopard-skin with a paper cup in hand. "Hey, you try this shit yet? It's weird." They backed away.

Better get some signs to put on these coolers, thought Roni. But first she'd try making an announcement. She spoke in an unnaturally loud voice that sounded strange to her.

"Hey, you guys? Everybody? Don't drink that stuff in the water coolers. They're decorations and might not be safe to drink. Tell anybody you see getting some, okay?"

People stared at her while she spoke, though a few nodded. The one with the Spock ears and paper cup both nodded and sipped. She couldn't help but feel maybe people were looking at her that way, like they didn't much understand what she was saying, because they were distracted by the mark on her face.

She decided she'd better go upstairs and talk to Hobie. That's where there might be some paper to make signs, anyway. She went up, knocked at the door, paused, opened it.

"Hobie, are you there?" The main room was dark, but the auditorium in the back showed a line of light under the door, and muffled voices were coming from it, like from a TV. She went up, knocked again, hesitated to open it. "Hobie? I have to talk to you."

Instead of answering, he chortled loudly. "Oh my God! Oh, that's beautiful!"

"Hobie?" she called again.

"Yes," came his voice from beyond the door. "Come in, come in."

She did, and saw that he was still in his pajamas, sitting in a chair and watching the news on TV. On the screen was a scene of the crowd outside the Mirror Theater, showing the mural with many people surrounding it, some of them holding signs, the only one of which she could read said "Christ Has Come."

Seated in another chair was Hobie's skeleton that he used to keep stuffed in a TV set at that video store he and Todd Dewolf had.

"It's going very nicely, isn't it, Veronica? I feel like I'm a real director at last."

"Hobie, things are getting out of control downstairs. Some people are drinking that pink stuff in the water coolers and throwing up. They think it's drinkable because of the coolers and cups and all."

"Good, very good. That's the intention."

"But people are puking. It seems to be getting them drunk or something. What's in it? You know you can't serve alcohol here, especially like that . . ."

He laughed. "Alcohol! Ah, that's rich. There's nothing to worry about. What's in those coolers is good for them."

"What?"

"What what?"

"What's in there that's good for them?"

"Water. What else?"

"What makes it pink?"

"Now, Veronica dear, you worry too much. If anyone asks, tell them that it's food coloring."

"Is it just food coloring? Food coloring doesn't make you puke."

"Yes. It's food and it's a color. The food is an old soft drink from Louisiana. It does have some special properties." He laughed.

"Okay, that's it. I'm going home. I don't want any part of this."

He became very serious. "No, you can't go. I need you here. You don't know how important you are to me, do you? You have no idea."

"At this point, I don't care, and besides . . ."

"Veronica, please listen to me. You know that I've changed, don't you? That's why there's this problem with Benny."

She wasn't going to mention Benny. "I think he's worried about you."

"Benny is a homosexual, and I'm not. Not anymore."

"You're not . . ." She hesitated. "A homosexual?"

He held up a hand, as if taking an oath. "I am no longer. My great mentor, Alberic Crabtree here, has shown me the way out of that trap." He gestured at the skeleton in the chair next to his. "And with the assistance of a few young women we engaged for the purpose. Professionals, of course. Never settle for an amateur when you can get a professional. Correct, Alberic?"

"You gave your skeleton a name?"

"Good heavens, no. He was named by his parents, over a century ago. I bought him online, believing him to be only an anonymous skeleton, and only gradually came to know his true identity as I learned to communicate with him. It was all intended to be. It's what's in those coolers that made it possible. Alberic's invention, you know. It opens the doors of perceptions as nothing else in this world can."

"The pink water is fucking LSD?"

"LSD! Did you hear that, Alberic? First alcohol, now LSD!" He reached over to the skeleton, put his arm around its bony shoulders and leaned his head against the rib cage, laughing heartily, as though the two of them were going into delighted hysterics together.

He stopped laughing abruptly, became very serious. "Forgive us, Veronica, we don't mean to laugh at you. It's just that misunderstandings about Verum Deus are insidious and multifold. I myself, along with many others, had the mistaken notion that a substance derived from Alberic's great creation was an improved version, cooked into an edible form often called worm. Indeed, there's currently a fashion for this concoction, which amounts to no more than yet another recreational drug, that is, a cheap high. Alberic has enlightened me on this score, that 'worm' is simply a distraction and, in effect, a deception. Verum Deus itself is the aged fermentation of Louisiana Bald Cat sarsaparilla, which Alberic predicted plainly back seventy some years ago, but flaws in the texts of his key works obscured this fact. I myself engaged Todd Dewolf to make some of this degraded version, and Benny tells me your silly husband, so very unworthy of you, is peddling it locally to the misinformed masses. In reality, aged Bald Cat itself is Verum Deus, and all you need do is *drink* it!"

As Roni stepped backwards away from him, Hobie rose from his chair, grasped each of her hands and gazed into her eyes. She glanced down at the front of his pants, poking out at her. She pulled her hands away, turning for the door. "I really have to go now. Sorry."

She was out in the hallway and headed down the stairs in moments.

25

TODD WAKES

Todd dragged himself out of a dismal bog of sleep that had rendered him too stupefied to dream. The bedsheets were damp and faintly foul, twisted over him like an ill-fitted strait-jacket. Beneath them, he was naked and alone. He rolled to one side, and his eyes went wide at the sight of several white maggots crawling over the edge of his pillow. He jounced up and fell out of bed.

After a moment, there were sounds coming from down the hall; someone was in the kitchen. Then steps, and Sky was in the doorway, looking fresh and clean with her hair wrapped up in a towel, in his big bathrobe, and carrying a mug. He smelled coffee. "Hey, you up? What are you doing on the floor?"

"I, uh, fell. When'd you get up?"

"Not long ago," she said, setting down the coffee mug. She sat on the bed, nuzzled her face against his face and tousled his hair. "Hey, you were incredible last night."

"I was—what happened?" He noticed a dark bluish mark under her left eye.

134

"You really don't remember? We were fucking like beasts. It was great."

"No, I mean, what happened to your eye?" He now vaguely remembered having sex with her, wasn't even sure it hadn't been a dream. But the sight of the bruise near her eye filled him with dread.

"It was an accident, my eye got in the way of your elbow at some point in the frenzy. Oh, my goodness." She got on her knees, put her arms around him and squeezed hard. She seemed awfully strong. He glanced at the pillow again, the maggots were gone.

"See how well those oysters work? Want some more for breakfast?"

26

JAIME AND CLARE, STILL ON THE ROAD

"So have you seen Todd's mural?"

"You mean the picture on the wall?"

"Yes, Todd's mural."

"Yeah. It looks like a man holding his hands up. People say it's Jesus, but, I dunno if it's him."

"But the spaceship that Todd painted is still there?"

"Yeah. Over him."

"And so this Qwiff just happens to show up when the image of Christ manifests on the wall that Todd had meant to use for his mural."

"Well, I don't know that she's a Qwiff or anything." He assumed this word meant slut.

"Oh, you don't think so? So you know who the Qwiff are?"

"No."

"That's right, you don't. You know what they really are? Not who, but what?"

"What?"

"Corpses. Corpses of beautiful women, reanimated to seduce men into having wild, depraved sex."

Jaime blanched, kept his eyes on the road.

"And this one has red hair, of course. Like his tattoo," she said.

"Whose?"

"Todd's tattoo."

"I never seen it."

"It's of a girl with red hair. The girl who's with him now. Obviously."

"Do they all have red hair?"

She laughed bitterly. "Why would that be?"

"Well, 'cause there was that other girl. She had red hair. Like the other one. Real red. Like . . . like blood."

Maybe he shouldn't have brought this up.

"What other girl?"

"I told you, the one that died. With red hair."

"Girl that died."

"In the woods, with Todd and Shannon. And Dewey."

"How do you know about such a thing?"

"I seen 'em. I happened to be running around there when they had her out in the woods."

"Had her . . . when was this?"

"Year ago."

"After I left?"

"Before."

"Out in the woods. And she died there?"

"Yeah." He didn't want to tell her more, not about what he did, and not about her being a victim of the Slasher, according to TV.

"I think you'd better tell me the whole story."

Jaime became flustered. "It was just, I was runnin' around and saw them. First Shannon was with her, then he got mad and was chasin' me, then Dewey was chasin' after Shannon, and that left Todd."

"You're saying they were fucking her."

"Yes, ma'am," he said in a low voice, remembering his brothers smacking him around for snitchin'.

"And Todd was with her when she died. Fucking her."

"I guess."

"How do you know she died?"

"I don't. I just seen her. Todd got up and ran away, and I seen her there."

"You saw her lying on the ground?"

"Yeah."

"Why do you think she was dead?"

"She was real dead. She rotted away." *Uh-oh, he shouldn't have said that. Now she might figure out the rest.*

"Awright, I understand now. So she's back."

"I don't . . . it can't be. I buried her." It occurred to him he hadn't been watching where he was driving and now didn't know where he was.

Clare clamped a hand onto his shoulder. "There's much more to this story, isn't there? And you're going to tell me the rest of it."

27

RONI AND THE SCREAMING CONTEST

R oni, stunned and completely at a loss about what to do, had returned to the ticket booth hoping to find Benny hanging around so she might confer with him about the stuff in the coolers and about Shannon. But he wasn't around, and Glenn was once again missing from the security desk. Nearly on autopilot, she went back to the auditorium looking for Glenn, on her way noticing the water coolers were gone. Had Glenn actually done something like his job and taken them away? She didn't know and wasn't sure she cared. She sat in the back row where she had previously found Glenn, eating popcorn, though this was quite forbidden.

The screaming contest was in progress, one of the audience-participation events at the marathon held between movies. The master of ceremonies for it was Billy from that awful local band Bearflesh that she'd seen a couple times at the Grasso Villa a few years ago. There had been three contestants screaming thus far, and two to go, and only one of them, the second one up, had been a guy. He had screamed louder than the girls, but the audience, mostly made up of guys, didn't seem to care much. They liked to hear girls scream instead, especially if they were cute.

The first had been a Heather type, little, fat and unappealing despite an obvious desire to please. Then came the guy. The next girl was better looking, though she sported a punk hairstyle Roni found very unbecoming. Her screaming had been kind of a raspy shriek, which brought some laughs, but sounded kind of pathetic.

The next one up was a toothy blonde with a '50s pinup figure, dressed in very unseasonal cutoffs with white frills as trim and a tied-off top open to show a great deal of cleavage. Roni could see how this was going to go.

Billy from Bearflesh—didn't everyone call them Beerflesh?—was dressed in worn-looking red spandex tights, stretched to their limit, and one of those long-sleeved t-shirts designed to look like a tuxedo, also at least two sizes too small for him and failing to cover his gut. But he did have a full and long mane of richly black and curly hair. Obviously a wig. He seemed to relish his role at this event.

"Awright, dudes and dudettes, next up, here she is! What be your name, doll-thang?"

She smiled toothily and swayed, the audience producing a low, amused murmur of aroused anticipation. "Destiny."

"Destiny! Awright, Destiny! Bitchin'name for a werewolf victim!" He put his arm around her and gave her a hug that was almost a mauling, which Roni could tell Destiny didn't like, but she smiled through it anyway. "Okay, Destiny, here's the scenario. You're running through the woods being pursued by the beast, and . . ."

Somebody touched Roni's shoulder. She looked up and saw it was Larry, the elderly and stoical projectionist, in his visor and shirt-sleeves. In keeping with his usual efficiency, he spoke quickly and plainly. "Hello, Roni. Ordinarily I wouldn't leave the booth while the movie's going, but I saw that you were in here, and something's up you should know about. Some police came into the booth just now, and wanted to know where Mr. Lautenschlager was. I told them probably up in his office. They didn't say anything about closing down the show, but they said they'd confiscated the water coolers in the lobby. They wanted to know what was in them, and I said I had no idea. Do you want to talk to them?"

"No. But thanks, Larry." She got up and left the auditorium as Destiny began her impressively loud and high-pitched scream. She would definitely win.

While Roni was hurrying upstairs, a bloated-faced boy dressed in a green vest and hat, apparently as a leprechaun, staggered near her and projectile-vomited onto the wall. He stood there before the result and seemed to be studying it. The vomit was a different shade of green than his costume. He held a paper cup crushed in his hand.

Once upstairs, she heard waltz music coming from Hobie's office. She pushed open the door and stepped in without knocking. She found Hobie dancing around the room with the skeleton, its feet tied to Hobie's own feet with twine. He was talking to it, but she couldn't hear what he was saying due to the loud music.

"For heaven's sake, turn that down! The police are here. They've taken the water coolers away. They're probably going to come up looking for you."

Hobie walked over to a boombox on his desk, turned off the music. "Just as you predicted, Alberic," he said to the skeleton. "I'd say it's time for us to make our exit, hmm?"

He turned to Veronica, kissed his fingers and made a tossing gesture. "Farewell, my sweet unrequited love and tormentor. You never knew, did you? Never suspected a thing. Well, them's the breaks. It's off to Thailand for Alberic and I."

Thailand? Before she could ask, he headed for the window, the skeleton now under his arm though still attached to his feet, and began to climb out of it.

"What are you doing?!" She ran to the window, looked out and saw him trying to grip a drainpipe. "For Christ's sake, you can't go down that. You'll fall!"

Hobie looked up, grinning, said, "Oh ye of little faith!" and removed one hand to make a salute. As he did, the pipe broke from the outside wall, bending and breaking off so he fell, hollering as he went down. He hit the ground with an appalling splat, at which his ample flesh seemed to burst around the sides and spread wider, gushing blood out of its edges. Lying there on the ground below, entangled with the skeleton and obviously dead, he seemed to be looking up at Roni.

She backed away from the window. The phone rang. In a daze, she answered it.

"Mirror Theater, this is Veronica."

The person on the other end spoke in a rapid, muffled voice. "You'd better clear that place out pronto, you heathens, because there's a bomb set to go off in five minutes that'll take the whole

144

building down! I mean it! The Lord is not mocked!"

Dial tone. Despite his attempt to disguise his voice, Roni could tell it had been Benny.

28

TODD AND SKY REACH A CLIMAX

By late afternoon Todd and Sky had fornicated more times than Todd could remember, and he was not tired, though she, while still affectionate and even gushy about his prowess, was gradually becoming less responsive. Though he seemed to possess a limitless amount of semen, Sky seemed to be running out of vaginal fluid. They'd resorted to employing some rather crusty old petroleum jelly they'd found in the bathroom cabinet. This had led to some further ideas of what uses it might be put to, which Sky had submitted to without objection, but perhaps not much enthusiasm. Todd noticed this, made note of it, but wasn't too worried about it. He was feeling really great, in fact.

They'd long since abandoned the bed for first the sofa in the living room, then the lounger for some fairly acrobatic deeds, and finally the open floor of the living room. For a while they had videos going, but they'd long since ended, and after a long period of letting the static run, they'd turned the thing off. That had been a couple of hours before.

Sky put her hands on his chest, as if holding him back. "Whoa! Let's take a break from it, tiger. Have a little quality time. I need to rest a little. I'm getting worn out." She ran her fingers over his hirsute chest. "My, you're hairy."

"Is that bad?"

"No, I like it, but I don't think I'd like any more than that." She touched his cheek. "Your beard grows really fast too. Huh. I need to get up, darling, please let me up."

"Okay, for a minute," he said, grinning. She smiled at him a bit weakly, put a long strand of hair behind her ear, studied him lying there on the floor. "How about some more wine?"

"Sure, I'll go get it." He leaped up.

"No, I will," she said.

While she was in the kitchen, Todd studied the backs of his hands. Actually, they did look a little hairier than he'd noticed before.

She came back out with two glasses of wine, clothed again in his robe, pulled tight around her, the belt cinched tight. They both drank, Sky standing against the wall, some distance from Todd.

"What day is it, do you know?" she said.

"I don't know. I don't keep track these days."

"It was Friday night when I came over."

"Then it's still Saturday."

"Wow, I've only been here a day. Seems like we've gotten to know each other so well in such a short time."

He laughed happily, but noticed the look on her face was rather sober and maybe a little anxious.

"You know, I'm going to have to be going pretty soon."

He was shocked. "Going? What do you mean?"

"I have to leave because, see, I'm supposed to visit my grandmother. That's why I was traveling this way. She asked me to visit. I haven't seen her in a long time."

"Let's go together."

She laughed briefly. "No, better not."

"I don't want you to leave."

"Aww. That's sweet, but I have to."

"You're going to leave me so soon? And after all . . . all this?"

"I'm going to visit my grandmother, and then I'll come back, okay?"

They stared at each other for a long moment. "No, Sky," Todd said finally. "No, it's not okay."

29

JAIME WITH CLARE SOME MORE

Jaime was driving pretty steadily, considering Clare had been weeping and, occasionally and without warning, striking him upside the head. "You thought she was really dead, didn't you? Just plain dead. Not that you'd be hard to fool."

"She was dead," said Jaime. "I didn't hurt her. She was already dead."

"You're a pig," said Clare. "You're lower than a pig. Pigs are clean compared to you."

Jaime knew this was unfair because he'd heard about how pigs would actually eat people, and not only when they were dead. He'd never heard about them rutting with people though, dead or otherwise, but he could see how they might. Dogs did, after all, at least with live people, like, humping on their leg and all that. He didn't think he'd done anything wrong, since the girl couldn't feel anything, but knew it wasn't the kind of thing you should tell anybody, and he wasn't going to admit it even though he'd kind of unintentionally already done so. Still, he was sweating with fear because Clare was

148

getting so crazy about it. She was crazy in the first place anyway, if she thought that girl was alive, even alive like a zombie is, or whatever she thought. *Why was she so mad anyway, if she thought they were evil?*

"Don't hit me no more. We'll go and find her and you'll see," he insisted. "We're almost there."

Clare had her head turned, looking out the window. She didn't speak for a while. But again, she turned abruptly and spoke furiously, as if her silences only allowed her furies to build. "So she was the perfect lover for you, wasn't she? You're with somebody, but you're still alone. Just a thing to play with. She was still warm, too, wasn't she?"

"It was cold out," said Jaime, then realized even that was more than he should say.

They finally reached the graveyard, and drove a ways into it, until the dirt road narrowed into a walking path crowded with trees. They stopped and got out, Clare now silent again, for some minutes, so Jaime worried the next fury would be far worse. The path petered out completely shortly after taking a turn, and Jaime worried he had chosen the wrong spot, but soon he saw the little cemetery ahead. There was still some light out, but dusk was beginning. He was pretty sure he remembered which spot he'd buried her in, over a ways beside that one gravestone that was bigger than the others and square like a cabinet rather than a plank of stone. Indeed, the outhouse was a short distance away. He hustled off toward it at a run.

"Hey!" said Clare. "Where you going? Don't run. You're not going to get away from me."

"I'm gonna get the shovel," he said, stopping and looking back. *What if he did run away? How would she stop him? It wasn't like she had a gun pointed at him.* Still, he had stopped running.

"What shovel?"

"It's in there," he said, pointing to the outhouse. "That's what I used when I buried her."

"Okay, go ahead."

He went into the old outhouse. It was still rank in there, but the smell was old and stale. The shovel, short and very rusted, its wooden post almost black with decay, was lying on the floor. He lifted it, showed it to Clare. "See?"

She nodded. "Get her, then." She said it like it was a challenge she didn't expect him to meet. In fact, Jaime was now worrying maybe he hadn't buried her deep enough and something had got her, like, maybe an animal dragged her away. Or maybe she'd just decayed away.

He looked around, couldn't find a spot that looked the same. He'd left a bunch of leaves over it, he remembered, but those were gone. Well, he guessed they would be. Afraid Clare would get mad again if he acted too uncertain, he started to dig right in front of him, hoping it would turn out to be the right spot.

The ground sure was hard. He could barely get the shovel to penetrate it. Would it have gotten that hard over the months since he'd buried her? Maybe, he didn't know.

Clare sat down on the ground and wrapped her arms around her knees, staring at him. She was motionless but didn't exactly look patient. He decided to try another spot but didn't say anything and, glancing back at her warily, it didn't seem Clare's expression had changed.

Jaime had dug in four different spots, and the sky had gotten a lot darker when she finally spoke. "You have no idea where she is, do you?"

"I think," he said, panting, his arms aching badly, "she must have rotted away."

"Decomposed," said Clare. "I don't think so." She got up and walked toward him, slowly.

"She was here but, you know, corpses rot away and stuff." He had a feeling one of Clare's furies was coming, a big one this time.

Still, she only walked, slowly, never taking her eyes from him. "Either that or she got up and walked away." This sounded to Jaime like she was being sarcastic, but he recalled what she'd said in the car, about the girl being alive.

"She was dead," said Jaime.

"I know," said Clare. "She was dead all along. That doesn't mean she didn't get up and leave after you buried her. Sounds like you didn't bury her very deep." In a quick gesture, she picked up the shovel, flew toward Jaime and battered him with it, first on his arm and shoulder and then aiming at his head. He covered his face with his hands and ran.

He heard a thud, looked back and saw, in the dim light, she'd thrown down the shovel. "C'mon," she said, "get back in the car and let's go. Let's go find her. She's with Todd."

Jaime wished he could run but was afraid she'd catch up if he did. "Don't you want to see the mural first?"

"I want to see her, if it isn't too late," said Clare. "C'mon, move it or lose it."

30

HEATHER AND FRED AT THE LIMBO WATCH TV

Heather mopped off the stuffed vinyl maroon barstools with a wet rag, a task Fred insisted she do before they open each day that she found pretty icky, just the thought of it really. People's butts on them. A TV news report on the Westside Slasher had ended, but there was nothing new in it.

"They may never catch him," said Fred. "Vicious criminals just disappear sometimes. Maybe Satan takes them in to serve in Hell. I recall that case up in Bethany some years back, that incestuous sister and brother who killed several people including their own mother and that young woman from TV, burned their own house down with the murdered bodies in it. It was all they wanted to talk about on the news for a while, but the police never found hide nor hair of either one."

"You know what I think," she said. "It's either Jaime Tales, Hobie Lautenschlager, or some other guy. Or Shannon Boner. He gets crazy sometimes."

"Hobie who?" said Fred.

"Lautenschlager. He don't come here. You don't know him. Real fat guy, thinks he's smart."

"Could be a woman doin' it," said Fred. "Women kill other women all the time, out of jealousy. Vanity and jealousy, they go together. In any case, it's someone you don't even know, girl. This ain't no small town."

"Hmm," went Heather, mildly annoyed. She thought, but didn't say, that it might also be Fred.

31

TODD BAILS OUT

Todd was sitting in the bathroom on the toilet, reading some more of the *Plan 666* book. He'd found an interesting passage about the "love bombing" practice:

"It was all about love, see," explained a girl who went by the name Breeze, who'd been engaged in the love bombing mission as early, she claimed, as age 13, and who spoke in the rather dated "hipster" slang typical of many Kindred members of all ages, in imitation of their founder, Daddy Dickey. "They said we were missionaries. They used to tell us a story in this like school we went to about a French saint named Julian. This Julian cat used to off animals and even his parents and all this bad shit. But then Jesus made his heart and he got turned on to love. Julian, after he got with love, used to carry people across a river, and one day this leper hits him up for a ride. I mean, you dig lepers, right? After that, the leper kept hitting him up for bread and food and shit, a place to crash, and Julian gave the leper whatever he asked for. Eventually the leper wanted to make it with him, and Julian was so into the love scene he did that too, and like, Julian was making it with this leper and in the middle of that the leper turned out to be Jesus, and took Julian to heaven with him. I mean, it's like an orgasm, it really shouldn't

just come from jerking off by yourself, right? It's a parable about giving, about love at a high level, a spiritual level. About how giving to others becomes giving to yourself, too."

"We didn't say love bombing among ourselves, we called it fuck fishing," said Cloud, an ex-Kindred member who'd gone on to work as an exotic dancer. "We weren't the only group like that doing it, but maybe we had more young girls, so it kind of got to be a big thing naturally, you know? Plus, I think we were pretty wily about it. They'd tell us to try and draw attention to ourselves but make it seem like we weren't, like were just naturally beguiling or whatever, innocently seductive. That is, assertive by being passive, you know? Because, you know, that is what really turns guys on. But you had to be careful because it's true what they say, that 'good men dream what bad men do,' you know? And once you bring that dream into reality, it can bring the bad out in them."

So she had to get out of there sometimes?

"Oh yeah," she said, "but also sometimes you can get past all that. You really have to play it by ear, or rather by eye, look them in the eye and try to see what's going on back there behind them. And like, it's best to get those things out of the way, to get past resentment and aggression and even hatred, to where that's exhausted. That's when love is possible, sometimes. But yeah, with some guys it got worse and worse, you couldn't get past it with them, and that's when it got dangerous, and you had to split."

Yes, he had to agree, there was some truth to that. More than a little. About some guys. Like himself. He picked up the nearly finished gallon bottle of Rhine Wine from the floor by the toilet and took a pull.

Sky called out from the next room. "Hey, Todd, are you in there?"

"Yes, why?"

"I miss you."

"I'll be out in a minute." He flushed the toilet, pulled his pants up and strode out. Funny, he used to be embarrassed about crude bodily functions around girls when he was younger. Didn't bother him at this point. In fact, nothing bothered him now.

He stepped into the bedroom. Sky lay there, glancing at him eagerly, her hands bound to the bedstead with some elastic bandages he'd found in the bathroom cabinet earlier. Her legs were free, pulled up. If he got close, he'd have to be careful to make sure she didn't kick him.

"Hey. It gets lonely out here like this. Can't see the TV, either."

"I know."

"Say, how about letting me loose here? Pretty please?"

"I'd like to but I don't trust you anymore."

"All I said was that I wanted to visit my grandmother."

"I'm not sure I believe you have a grandmother. What's your grandmother's name?"

"Evelyn. Why don't you believe me?"

"Because I think you just came here because of this Kindred thing."

"Do what?"

"That's what they call it in the book."

"What book?"

"This cult called the Kindred. You were in it, weren't you? In California?"

She hesitated. "I was, but I'm not now."

"Why not?"

"I quit. That's all. I'm on my own now."

"Well, it doesn't matter, I guess."

"Really, this is awfully uncomfortable. I don't mind kink, it's fun sometimes, even when it's rough. But you know, enough is enough. Back to ordinary life." He noticed the bruises around her neck, bad in spots, purple blotches, slightly swollen even. His doing.

He said, "See, that's just it, that's what I can't get back to. I mean, it's not your fault. It's what happened before. I've got something really wrong with me. A screw loose."

"No you don't."

"You know it's true. I'm dangerous. You're scared of me, in fact."

"I'm not scared of you at all."

"You should be, and I think you are."

"You're not that bad. I've seen worse. You just need to modify a little. Don't get so carried away. And that's not why I said I was leaving."

"No, see, you've seen worse but I have too. I've seen worse from me. I wasn't sure about what had happened, but now I am."

"I don't know what you're talking about."

"There's no way you would." He sighed. "It's funny, you know, I always thought I'd reach this point and it would be all dramatic and emotional. But there's nothing. I guess that's what it's about. Nothing. Zero."

"If you let me go—"

"I gotta go find something." He got up and went to the dresser across from the bed, opened a drawer and got out one of his old switchblades.

"What are you looking for?" Sky sounded afraid.

He brought the switchblade over, and her eyes froze upon it. "You're not the first girl I messed up," he said. "I think I killed a girl in the woods last year. I was fucking her and I strangled her."

"You wouldn't ever do that," said Sky, but her voice was wavering.

"I might have killed some more," he said. "Here, let's see."

He put the blade against her throat—she shut her eyes hard, held utterly still—then ran it along a cheek of her pretty, angelic face. He pressed the tip of the knife in near her mouth, feeling his dick get hard. She whimpered as a trickle of blood slid down unto the pillow.

"Don't worry, it's okay." He stepped away. "That's what I wanted to know." *Where had he put that damned thing?*

He found the shotgun in the front closet, yanked it out and returned to the bedroom. When Sky saw what he was carrying, she trilled in fear.

"I said don't worry." He put the shotgun under his arm, flicked opened the switchblade again with his other hand. Her eyes went immediately to that. He dug at the bond on her left hand, cut through it, did the same with the other. She tumbled off the bed, into a corner of the room. "What—"

"Just stay there," he said. He went into the bathroom, closed the door.

"What are you doing?" she called.

He looked at himself in the mirror. Hollow-eyed, dead-tired looking, jaw hanging slack, a dewlap developing under his chin. Thirty-nine years old. Never wanted to be forty anyway.

He put the barrels under his chin, wondered if it would hurt.

"Todd?"

He heard the blast for a bare moment. *Ye—*

32

SHANNON AND DEWEY GO TO TODD'S

"How does your grandma even drive this fucking car?" said Shannon.

"She doesn't drive it very much. It's better than nothing."

"I wouldn't be fucking caught dead in it."

"Well, you're in it now." Dewey decided that if Shannon was going to be this shitty, he might as well speak up. "Don't you think we ought to tell Todd about his car getting ripped off?"

"No, because I want to get it fucking back and tell him after. We know what retard fucking took it."

"I think we ought to tell him. It's his car."

"Yeah, it's his car, and after a while, once I start making more money, I'm getting another car anyway. Fuck this borrowing somebody's car and then somebody steals it."

"How you gonna make money?"

"There's money in selling worm, man. That's why we're doing it, right?"

We, thought Dewey, *he hadn't said anything about cutting me in.* "We haven't made much yet."

"That's 'cause we're just getting started."

"I'm not sure it's such a good idea anyway."

"Now you're gonna bitch about it, huh?"

"No, I'm just saying, the shit is bad for you and you can probably get in real bad trouble for selling it."

"What do you mean? It's not even illegal so far as we know."

"I bet it is illegal, plus it's bad for the people you're selling it to."

"Well, what, am I making them take it?"

"You're enabling them to take it."

"Enabling. Is that a word you heard on TV?"

"Everybody says that. That's what it is. We did the shit ourselves and agreed we wouldn't ever take it again."

"Well, we're not 'everybody,' are we? Kids want to do it, so let them. I didn't say I wouldn't take it again because I thought it was heavy or scary or some shit. I just thought it wasn't much. It's like speed or something. Less than speed, more like Jolt Cola or some shit."

"It's a little more intense than Jolt Cola," said Dewey.

"It's like shooting a couple Jolt Colas. That's about it. It's just hyped right now. We're just meeting demand. If you're so against it, why didn't you say anything before?"

"I'm just saying I think Roni's going to be worried now that she knows about it."

"How the fuck does Roni know about it?"

"Heather said she was there when those kids asked for you, so she does know."

"She doesn't know what it is or what they were looking for me for. I told her I was going to manage their band."

"Why would they want you for that?"

"Well, they were going to the Grasso, so maybe they were going to have a retro headbanger group. Might be the latest thing for the younger set. So, I'm well familiar with the shit they're after, maybe."

"Man, they didn't go there, that's where you got the place wrong. Don't you even remember that, from yesterday?" *Maybe shouldn't have said that*, Dewey thought, *but sheesh.*

"I'm not thinking about it. I got other stuff on my mind right now. Jesus fuck, will you get off my back?"

"Awright, I'm sorry. I'm just pissed off about everything today, same as you. So where are we fucking going anyway?"

"I guess let's go tell Todd what happened. What the fuck. See how he's making out with the chick."

When they got to Todd's house, both of them went up to his door to knock. There was no answer. After a minute, they knocked again. They could hear somebody moving around in there. The door opened, and Sky was there, wearing a bathrobe that must have been Todd's. Her eyes looked funny, woeful, and one had a bruise around it.

"Hi," she said, sullen.

"Hey," said Shannon, acting cheerful. "Is old Todd home?"

"No. He's asleep."

"Well, like, we wanted to talk to him about something."

"I can't— I don't want to try and wake him up," she said.

"Huh. Well, when he does wake up, will you tell him we were looking for him?"

"Okay." She seemed aggravated or something, didn't want to talk. She barely glanced at Dewey, but seemed to watch Shannon warily.

"So, how's things going?" said Shannon.

"Okay."

"You . . . you guy's gettin' along okay, you and Todd?" Shannon grinned.

"Uh-huh," she said, unsmiling.

"You sure? You seem a little . . ."

She tossed her hair as if impatient. "Everything's fine."

Her eyes said otherwise, Dewey thought.

"Okay, well, I guess we'll see you around then. Don't forget to, uh, tell Todd we stopped over, need to tell him something."

"Okay. Bye." She closed the door quickly.

They walked back to the Chevy. "What was that about?" said Dewey.

"Fuckin' women, man," shrugged Shannon, as they climbed back in.

Dewey glanced up at the sky. It was getting dark pretty fast. As they drove off, he said, "You noticed the eyes, right?"

"Yeah, the black eye. I saw it."

Dewey meant more than that but let it go. "You don't think he's getting freaky with her, do you?"

"I dunno," said Shannon. "I wouldn't think so, but he has gotten to be a porn freak, I guess."

33

JAIME AND CLARE FIND TODD

"You want me to go up there with you?" Jaime said.

"Of course, you're the one who started this."

Jaime was going to say "I didn't start it" but didn't want to get hit again. He also didn't really want to confront Todd or see the girl again. He felt a little guilty, as always, for being a snitch—in the presence of people he'd snitched on, anyway. But he figured they'd all be more interested in each other than in him, and he could probably lam out of there pretty fast after the door opened.

They knocked. Nobody answered. Knocked again. The door, unlocked, came open.

They went inside. There were clothes strewn over the furniture, dishes and empty wine bottles scattered around, VHS tapes too, and a lamp lying on its side on the rug. There was something ominous about the place, almost an odor, that disturbed him. He thought it might have actually been a sex smell, since he figured they'd been fucking a lot. When he peeped at her she was probably having a shower because they'd just had sex, or were about to, or whatever.

But no, it was something else, something real bad.

"Todd?" called Clare, her voice rising as she stretched the word. She headed off down a hallway, and after a moment of indecision, Jaime hurried along behind.

They stepped into a bedroom in the back. It was even more of a mess than the living room. The bedclothes were in disarray, and a drawer in the dresser was pulled out and its contents spilled. They moved closer to the bed, there was a red blotch on the pillow, a blood stain. Clare stepped into the bathroom. It was through this bathroom window where Jaime had watched the girl showering until she'd noticed him and screamed. He was thinking about that scream, which had made him run away, when another, more piercing scream came from inside the bathroom, so loud and sustained it seemed as if it might shatter that window and all the windows in the house.

Terrified, he ran up to the door to see. There was much more blood, splattered across the walls and mirror and dripping from the sink. Someone lay twisted up in the center of the floor, gooey red smears all over and under them and everywhere. Clare, still screaming, turned and elbowed Jaime out of her way as she exited the room. As she did, he briefly saw an object in her hands that, for a moment, he thought was part of a large doll. Outside the room, her screams collapsed into heaving sobs.

He stared at the person on the floor. It didn't have a head. Its neck was a band of skin raggedly torn at the rim. The neck contained gnarled red meat surrounding a lumpy whitish stick in its center. Bone. It protruded a little above the meat. A blood-streaked axe leaned against a side wall.

He hurried out, his stomach churning, fell to his knees and nearly onto his face, his insides pulsing as vomit raged out of his mouth and spilled onto his legs. Looking up moments later, he saw Clare, quiet now, sitting at the edge of the bed, holding Todd's gruesome severed head right before her face, looking straight at it and, rather calmly, talking to it.

"You wouldn't ever listen to me, would you? You were so stable and smart and I was supposed to be crazy, wasn't I? There weren't any Gnoomes or Qwiffs. It was ridiculous. Well, look who was right and who was wrong."

Clare didn't glance at Jaime and seemed to have forgotten he was there. She didn't even turn to look as he stumbled to his feet, ran from the room and out the front door.

34

RONI AND THE GIRL SCOUTS

Roni was at home, having run all the way there from the theater. Once inside, she fell into an armchair, hyperventilating for some minutes. Her breath having settled down, she stared at the wall, whimpered for a while, then got one of Shannon's Mexican beers out of the refrigerator. There were three, and she drank the first two rather quickly, and was now nursing the third.

She wondered where Shannon was. Probably still looking for his stupid car. Which wasn't even his. If he came home, he'd be pissed she drank his beers. But who cared. God, here she was thinking about her fucked-up marriage when Hobie was dead and the whole fucking town had gone insane. She felt kind of like she was 'luded out, like in the old days. Only worse. It wasn't the beer. It was like being a head on a post. Numb. Like Thorazine was supposed to be, or what she'd heard of it.

"People react in different ways to the revelation that nothing means anything because everyone will eventually die and then nothing will matter," Hobie had said. Maybe so. Maybe she should turn on the TV and look at that instead of at the wall. Not that it was all that different. It just moved around more and had people in it.

She thought of Hobie going out the window, the smile on his face, and started to sob, though she did not feel sad, exactly. It all seemed so faraway, as though it had happened years before. Still, the fact she had some sort of emotional response reassured her somewhat, though she only sobbed a couple of times and then became utterly numb again. Maybe she was in shock. That was probably it.

Oh yeah, was going to turn on the TV. She saw the remote on the end table, stared at it for a minute or so. *Okay, TV.* She picked up the remote and pressed the button, and it came on to a home shopping network channel. Good grief, had she been watching this?

She went through the channels until she found a news report, caught in midstream, the Mirror showing on the screen, with emergency vehicles on the sidewalk in front of the place, lights flashing, and much yelling and crying going on, though the people standing around and crowded by the vehicles all looked lethargic, empty-eyed. The way she felt, more or less.

The girl reporter on the screen, however, speaking into a microphone outside the theater, sounded frantic.

"—died immediately, according to reports, when he leaped from a window to avoid arrest. Police confiscated the dispensers of the strange pink liquid thought to contain a dangerous recreational drug that has apparently sparked the melee—"

On impulse, Roni changed the channel. "Let's see what else is on," she said aloud, then laughed. Why was she laughing?

Switching through the channels again, she stopped at the image of that old bastard evangelist guy, Dr Trumpet something, holding forth as always. *Did this fucker ever shut up? Or go home?*

"—because atheism is Satan's most useful tool of all. What do people have to fear in a world where death is the end of everything, where no reward or punishment can take place? What to fear but death itself, even as they know they'll not even feel regret once it's come to them. For the atheist, and for their lord Satan, each death is the end of the world. The paradox, my friends, is that the escape from judgment is at once the most fearful fate conceivable and a license to commit any crime one might believe they can get away with in pursuit of profit or sensation. And what if this nihilism of ultimate oblivion is brought to its ultimate conclusion: why even fret over earthly punishments, if only a void awaits?"

167

"To keep from going into that void for as long as possible, dumbass, I would think," said Roni to the TV. She hit the off button, stared at the blank screen. But funny thing, it wasn't entirely blank. She could see her own image in it, vaguely.

She got out of the armchair and crawled across the floor to peer closely at her dim reflection in the screen. Were those shadows or her mark, expanded more than ever? It looked as though almost half her face was black. In fact, the mark seemed to spread even as she held very still and studied her dark reflection. She began again to sob, then, surprising herself, to shriek. She put her hands over her mouth to stop herself. The sound continued. It wasn't her after all.

There were sirens, coming nearer, down the street outside. They became very loud and then shut off abruptly, close by. She tensed. Police.

She heard someone outside. There was a knock at the door. "Who is it?" she called out.

"Girl Scouts!" came mingled, high-pitched voices. Little girls.

She laughed again, went to the door and opened it. Three girls in uniforms, berets and sashes, with a woman, someone's mom, all smiling for a beat or two. One began, "Hello, would you like to—" when all their eyes froze upon her face. The scouts looked amazed and horrified. The mom, instead, looked surprised, embarrassed, pitying. "I'm sorry to bother you, we're just, we're selling Girl Scout cookies, and—"

"No thanks," said Roni, slamming the door. No, she would not look in the fucking mirror, or even at the TV. She sat back in the armchair with her hands over her eyes, envisioning Hobie's burst-open corpse staring at her, enduring the image.

35

CLARE ARGUES WITH TODD'S HEAD AND PICKS UP A HITCHHIKER

Clare carried Todd's head out to the car, which was parked in front of the house. She opened the front side door and put the head on the seat, and went around to get in the driver's side. She turned the key, which Jaime had left in the ignition, and the motor started.

"Are we going for a ride?" Todd said.

"Yes, we're going to go see the manifestation of our Alien Lord Jesus Christ at the movie theater, if we can get through the crowd."

"Hoo boy, there's a crowd?"

"It was pretty thick when we passed by there before."

"Where'd Jaime go, by the way?"

"I don't know or care."

Clare hadn't driven in a while and found the big car rather hard to maneuver. Todd's head sat on the seat next to her, gore seeping out from his neck. She'd been slightly surprised when he began to answer her back, at first in murmurs but then in full sentences. Soon the dead would be out of their graves for Resurrection. Could be Todd was an early bird.

Being Todd, he was as snarky as ever, though sometimes he would fall silent for long stretches. But then, it was also like Todd to pretend he didn't hear her when she was pointing out something to him he didn't want to acknowledge. It might be partly because he was embarrassed to have fucked up so badly, but he could at least admit she'd been right all along.

"She was a long-haired redhead, wasn't she?" Of course she was. Busty, long-legged, and dumb, that's what he went for. Giggled a lot, probably. Every time they'd go out in the old days, if there was a redhead like that somewhere, he'd fix on her and moon. Especially if the slut was walking around and wiggling her butt. That always got him. Of course, the Qwiff assigned to seduce him would take the form of a bimbo of the type he went for. Clare felt sorry for him, but the fact he wasn't responding to her question was starting to make her really mad.

"So, was it fun? Your little wild time with Red? Did the carpet match the drapes? Or wasn't there a carpet?" She didn't mean to say that vulgar thing, it just slipped out.

"Don't be vulgar," he said. "You and your old hangup about red-headed girls." His voice was distant, and his mouth didn't move. Well, at least that got him to talk.

"I told you this was going to happen, didn't I? But no, I was crazy. That wacky Clare. She always was nuts, but she really went bonkers when she got into UFOs."

"I never said that," said Todd.

"But you thought it, didn't you? Like I didn't know what you thought. Well, you're going to see how right I was about everything." She feared for a moment he might mention the baby, but no, he wouldn't. Wouldn't dare.

"What do you mean? Where are we going?"

"Haven't you heard about the big event down at the Mirror?"

"The marathon?"

"No, not the marathon! The manifestation! The one I told you was coming."

"You mean . . . the big J?" It was just like him to say something sarcastic in a real deadpan way like that.

"His name is Jesus Christ, and yes, that's what I mean. His image manifested on your mural."

"You mean . . . on the wall there? With the flying saucer?"

170

"It's right underneath the flying saucer. That's why you couldn't finish it. It was going to be finished for you."

"I couldn't finish fucking anything." His usual self-pity, but somehow there was a finality to it now that hadn't been there before.

"Well, you should see it now. In fact, we're going to, that's where we're going."

"I'm not going to be able to see it. I'm dead."

"Oh, shut up! If you're dead, how come you're talking to me?"

"Clare. You'd better not take me there and be seen carrying me around and talking to me in public."

"Why not?"

"Because I'm a fucking severed head and I'm dead. They'll put you in the looney bin for good this time."

"I don't care, because Jesus is back, like I told you, though you won't even admit that I was right."

He sighed. "What you told me was some crazy shit about UFOs and aliens who try to eat your brain or something." This made her angry again because it was exactly what he had said before she left.

"Your brain," she sneered, imitating his lazy drawl. "Eat your brain. I never said any such thing." It occurred to her he now had a big hole in his skull, and in fact, glop that was presumably brain matter was dripping out of his head, partly because he was leaning at an angle with the hole turned downward.

She righted it. That was only his physical brain anyway, not his spiritual mind. But all at once, she felt terrible and stifled a sob. She decided she should still be mad at him, though.

"So was it fun while it lasted, debauching your little demoness from Hell?" She felt this was a little nasty even as she said it.

"Look, what did you expect? I was lonely."

She was about to say something about how he had Hobie Lautenschlager's porno movies to keep him company, but that seemed pretty nasty as well. She glanced down at him again but found she had to look away so she wouldn't whimper. The wound in the side of his head was hideous, and the gore leaking from the jagged bottom of his neck was now dripping down the front of the car seat. She really ought to have looked for some kind of container to carry him in.

"I suppose it's all my fault then," she said.

"I never said it was your fault." That was true, he hadn't come out and said it, exactly. But she knew he'd thought it.

"I left because I couldn't stand it anymore. Couldn't stand seeing what you were doing to yourself. Destroying yourself and destroying me too."

"I don't blame you for leaving. I never did. Okay?"

Just as Clare was about to answer, she saw a girl standing by the side of the road, up ahead. The girl was slender, wore a tight black dress with black fishnet hose and had spiky black hair. Clare thought right away she could be a witch and maybe from A.O.A. She could even be the Qwiff herself in disguise. Her hair could be dyed. In fact, it looked dyed, it was too black. Though as they drew closer, it became plain she wasn't busty but had little a-cup breasts at best. She might even be someone Clare was intended to meet at this important juncture.

"Why are you slowing down?" said Todd's head.

"That girl hitchhiking," she said. "Is that her?"

"I can't see anybody."

"I'm going to pick her up."

"Don't pick up hitchhikers, for Christ's sake."

"Don't blaspheme."

She pulled over and stopped by the girl, who didn't smile or nod, but just opened the front passenger door. Todd sighed, but didn't say anything more.

Seeing the head on the seat, the girl hesitated. Clare thought she might scream, but instead she shrugged, closed the door, opened the door to the back seat and got in.

"Thanks," the girl said, and plunked down. "Wow, a four door. Don't see these very much anymore."

Clare started down the road again. She was sorry she'd picked her up because now she was reluctant to talk to Todd in front of her. It hadn't occurred to her before that this would be a problem. In fact, though she'd picked the girl up partly to spite him, he may have urged her not to because he figured it would come out this way, and he wouldn't have to talk. In fact, when she glanced down at him, his face seemed to bear the trace of a smirk.

"So who's your friend?" said the girl from the back, calmly.

"My ex," said Clare.

"Ha-ha! Yeah. I guess so."

"Actually, we're just separated, not divorced."

"So where are we going?"

"We're heading downtown."

"Great, that's where I'm going." The girl leaned back and

172

hummed to herself, pulled a compact out of her pocket, opened it and waggled her head around, looking at herself in the compact's mirror. She wore a lot of make-up, the same as any slut did.

"Hey, my name's Meg," said the girl, putting her compact away, pulling a cigarette from her purse and lighting it. "What's yours?"

"Clare. Have you heard about the manifestation?"

"What do you mean?"

"At the movie theater."

"At the Mirror? You mean the picture on the wall? Yeah, I already saw it. It's a hoot."

"It's an image of Christ," Clare said. "It portends his return from a faraway galaxy where he's been imprisoned until an army of the Elect was assembled to set him free."

"Sounds like *Star Trek*. He sure picked a shithole building to put his picture on," said Meg.

"Well, it's because it was Todd's mural."

"Who's Todd?"

"This is Todd right here. Todd, aren't you going to say hello?"

"The head? Ho ho!" said Meg. "Hi, head! What'd you say his name was, Todd? Where'd you get that thing, anyway? It's cool, it almost looks real."

"Better leave the discussion right there," said Todd. The girl didn't seem to hear him. Maybe only Clare could hear him. He might be right. No, no more pretending, the Coming was nigh, and she was going to tell the world the way things really were.

"It is real," said Clare. "They tried to destroy him, but they were too late. The Resurrection of the Dead is underway."

"Are you into Wicca or something?"

"No."

"No? But that's some shit about Samhain or whatever you're talking about, right?"

"Certainly not," said Clare.

The girl tossed her cigarette out the window. "This one guy I was running around with, Tyler, is into all that too. He's a real asshole. I'm going to kill him and Ryan when I find them. Fuckers, taking off without me just 'cause I fell asleep."

"Today is the start of the end of everything," said Clare.

"Is that kind of like 'today is the first day of the rest of your life,' only bad?" asked the girl.

"That's why His image has appeared," said Clare.

"But doesn't that shit happen all the time? I mean, a stain gets on a silo or some shit and somebody says it looks like Jesus. Then a bunch of hillbillies come and gawk at it and get all excited, and it gets on the news."

Clare was only mildly annoyed by these ignorant comments. "No, it isn't like that. There are those among us who want to prevent it from happening, who want to drag the whole world down to their level by spreading cynicism, by seducing the unwary—"

"Oh yeah, I know about them. They're all over the place."

"You know about the Gnoomes?"

"No, never heard about that, but there was this one guy I was living with for a while. And he was like trying to use drugs to try and fuck me. He wasn't dosing me or anything, just thought I'd be grateful for getting high. But I wasn't that grateful, ha! 'Cause he was this real old guy, but he was like an old hippie, so he thought he was still cool and shit. You know, that's how they are. He was giving me this weird drug that was supposed to make me his slave or some shit. I do like to get high, but I figured out what was going on because he started trying to order me around, like he was going to pimp me out. But it didn't work the way he wanted, not on me. Asshole."

"You were very lucky," said Clare, "because that was a Gnoome. I'm surprised you got away. Maybe a Niff intervened on your behalf. There is a drug the forces of evil are employing now to try and enslave young women."

"Oh, yeah, that's what they want. It's like white slavery in the old days. I mean like, this guy was weird but he was like a lot of, you know, regular guys. He didn't just want to get into my pants, he wanted me to really like him, but I guess he thought that was the way to do it. At first, he was just trying to fuck me, but then I like got to him, I guess. Did you ever see the movie *White Zombie*?"

"No," said Clare.

"I have," said Todd, but the girl didn't seem to hear him.

"It's a real cool old movie, like from a hundred years ago, where this girl gets made into a zombie by this guy—"

"There's a drug being distributed very widely today that's intended to make the entire population of the world into zombie-like creatures of a sort."

"You don't mean worm, do you? Some people say you should call it vee dee, but that sounds like venereal disease."

"It is called that, though it's real name is Verum De—"

"Oh shit, I did some of that last night! I don't think it's the same as what this hippie guy was giving me. Either that or this stuff we had last night wasn't very good. It just made you feel, like, wound up but really useless. I mean, Ryan liked it, but he would. Tyler said he thought it was okay. It wasn't like that other drug I was talking about. That was a pill you swallowed. This was stuff you eat and it looks like gummy worms. That's why people call it worm."

"You took Verum Deus." Clare sounded very serious.

"Yeah, if that's vee dee. Why, does it fuck you up? I do feel a little strung out still. Guess that's why I'm babbling."

"It will take over your entire mind and soul as time goes on."

"Omigod, don't tell me shit like that. Where'd you hear that? You sound like Dr. Trumpetface or whatever."

"It's in the—"

"I'm not taking any more of it anyway. I don't need to be doing that shit. I need to get another waitressing job, and I can't work if I'm strung out. I was going to stay with Tyler at his crib, but now he says he's moving back in with his parents, the little homo."

"Don't worry, it doesn't matter."

"Doesn't matter? It matters to me."

"Everything will change, starting today. You won't need a job."

"Yeah, I don't know how I'm going to eat or where I'm going to live. I was living in my car for a while, but then I had this stupid accident and it got totaled."

"You can have this car if you like, but you're not going to need it."

"Huh?"

"I said, you can have this car."

"Are you shitting me?"

"No, take it. This is where we get off." Clare stopped, pulled out the keys and handed them to her, grabbed the head and jumped out.

"Jesus, that thing looks real," said Meg.

"Yes, it's all real. Don't blaspheme," said Clare as she walked away.

36
FRED'S DREAM

Fred was taking a nap on the cot he kept in the back room at the Limbo before it was time to open. More and more, he didn't like to stay at home. His wife had died two years before, and he didn't feel as comfortable there by himself, and tended to get depressed on days when he was home. He had the radio on, tuned to a country music station that still played real country music, oldies they called them, from the '60s or earlier, rather than the kind that sounded like rock and roll to him. He was half-awake and noticed when an old Kitty Wells record came on, "It Wasn't God Who Made Honky Tonk Angels" and was slightly annoyed when his mind conjured images of girl angels with blonde ringlets in long white gowns playing guitars. He didn't really believe angels looked like that, maybe this popped up when he was on the edge of dreaming because of those old turn of the century pictures of angels Grandpa still had in his house, adorable girls in pious poses with superimposed wings, rolling their big eyes heavenward, all a little on the young side. But abruptly the song was replaced with a news report, and he heard a frantic announcer say something like "The White House itself has now confirmed that millions have disappeared throughout the world, especially in the US. Newborns in maternity wards were the first reported disappearances . . ."

He rose up from the cot. Was the radio even on? No. Must be the TV in the barroom. Now he could definitely hear something, but the sound was different, loud laughter and whistles, excited people acting up, sounded like. *Was it the TV or real people?* He stepped into the next room, found they were open already, three regulars hanging around— Roy, Clayton and old Vincent Peterman, who was always already three sheets to the wind—when he came in the door. "Uh oh, there he is," said one.

Fred looked at the screen, which showed a gauzy scene of a nearly naked female couple in bed, squirming together. "What the— Who put on this filth?"

"We changed it to that," said Roy mischievously. "We figured you was asleep. Go ahead and change it back. We knowed ya would."

Fred did so, switching to the Landfrey channel, which showed an image of a giant bloodied fetus holding a giant dime, which turned out to be a picture on the side of a van. "Aw, shit," muttered Roy, and the old drunk Vincent added, "Boys, that was just gettin' hot."

Fred noticed Heather wasn't there. "Heather! Where in the doggone is that girl?"

"She ran down to the big party up the street," said Clayton. "It's gettin' all outta control, she got all excited seeing it on TV. Be there or be square."

37

CLARE THROWS THE HEAD

As Clare approached the theater on foot, intrigued with the assembled crowd and both thrilled and frightened at the prospect of seeing the image of Christ, on which so much depended, she didn't even want to talk to Todd anymore, but he kept rattling on to get her goat, acting all blasé but really wanting to start something, like in the old days.

"So you're way into the big J now, huh? It used to be just UFOs."

"In the first place," she said, keeping her voice even to deny him the pleasure of thinking he'd upset her, "'Big J' is blasphemy, but you can be very sure Christ doesn't care a bit what you say about Him. Furthermore, 'UFO' isn't an accurate term when a flying vessel has been identified by experts as a ship that could not be from the Earth."

"I stand corrected," said Todd. So typical of him to be sarcastic when he couldn't counter points she'd made.

"I'm bringing you here because something is happening I think you should see. You've screwed everything up like you always did, let some big-butt redheaded Qwiff trick you into losing your head, but

178

His grace is so great, you may still be redeemed."

"Redeemed from what? I'm dead. You got a way out of that?"

"If you're so dead, why do you keep talking to me?"

"I don't, except in your mind."

"Oh, that's right, I'm crazy! You go right back to that old line because you think it bothers me. I couldn't care less that you say that."

"Severed heads don't talk. If you hear me talking, that must be because you're crazy."

"Then stop talking so I won't be crazy. Sounds like you want me to be crazy. You always wanted that."

"Why the hell would I? You think I wanted everything to end up like this?"

"You wanted that Qwiff to show up, didn't you? You'd been developing her in your mind for years. Finally she was finished and they let her out, to take you."

"Who did what?"

"The Gnoomes, as you know very well."

"The Gnoomes and the Qwiff? This comes from that Delbert lunatic, right? The UFO abductee guy?" She wasn't going to respond.

After a few moments, Todd started in again. "You used to call them 'the Space Brothers.' Is this the same bunch, the Gnoomes? I thought they were good guys. Our guardian angels who watch over us and all that."

"You never paid attention to what I tried to explain to you. The space brothers were the Niff, not the Gnoomes. The Gnoomes are criminals who were exiled to Earth by the Niff millions of years ago. They live in the center of the Earth, and they do more than watch us, and no, they don't mean us well. They're here to hold us down, to destroy any prospect of good things, of things being as they should. The Niff, under Christ's command, seek to defend us against them."

"Huh. This is new. You didn't think that before, did you?"

"I've done a lot of study and learned some things since I left. A lot of what I used to think was wrong. It came from the Kindred group, whose revisionist leader had intentionally misrepresented the truth."

"I see. The truth at last, eh? From Delbert, the escaped mental patient."

"That's right, be sarcastic! Everything is shit to you. And that's just . . . that's what they want people to think about him." The theater was now only a block away. Clare stepped faster.

179

"Okay, whatever you say. What are we going to see here?"

"I told you. Your mural."

"What mural?"

On the wall of the Mirror, the movie theater."

"I didn't get it finished. It just had a little flying saucer up in the corner."

She heard chanting in the distance but couldn't make out what was said, except for the word "Jesus."

"It's been finished for you. Or rather, you finished it without knowing."

"Wasn't there a fairy tale like this once, something about a shoemaker and elves?"

"You'll find out soon enough. Look, there it is, right there!" Turning the corner, she saw the wall for the first time, surrounded by a noisy, chattering crowd of people, some of them holding placard signs, and among them a few mobile vans with TV station logos on their sides and what looked like satellite dishes on their roofs. Bright lights from poles shone unto the wall, which bore a rough image of a face with a nose and one eye behind what could be seen as heavy dark brown hair and a beard and, above it, two appendages of unequal width and length that might be uplifted arms in approximately the right place to be attached to a body beneath the head, represented by a white field that could conceivably be part of a robe. Above the figure and to one side was a far more focused and clearer picture of a silver flying saucer.

"It's real! I knew it was!" Clare fell to her knees and elbows, clunking the head against the ground.

"Hey, watch it!" said Todd.

She raised Todd's head up, holding it so he could see the mural. "There! See? I told you!"

"No, actually, I can't see anything. I'm dead, you know? Eyes don't work anymore when you're dead."

She was exasperated. "That's funny, your mouth sure works."

"So you say." Now he was trying to sound like he was bored.

"Let's get closer," she said. "I want to see!" She started to run in the direction of the wall, tripped and fell, lost her grip on Todd's head. It rolled forward and bounced against a standing girl's ankle. The girl, in cutoffs and a halter top, apparently a marathon-goer rather than a Christian, looked down, said, "What the fuck? Yuck!" and gave the head a kick. It rolled farther, and Clare dashed forward to catch and lift it.

"That was close," said Todd. "She might have seen what I am. Not from a novelty shop."

"It doesn't matter," said Clare.

"It'll matter when they come after you. You know they'll put you in a mental ward and not just for observation like before."

"I don't care. It doesn't matter. Don't you see, everything is different now. It's because of your mural. You were chosen to make it, and now—"

"I wasn't going to make a mural with a weird distorted picture of Jesus on it. It was supposed to be a bunch of characters from science fiction and horror movies."

"A minute ago you said you couldn't see it," she pointed out. She had him there, and he didn't respond. "Don't think you can undo Christ's return with his army of Niff to defeat the Gnoomes by being cynical about it, even if He did pick your mural to appear on."

"I wouldn't dream of it," said Todd. Sarcastic again.

"You'd like to make it all go away, wouldn't you? You've always been self-defeating and self-destructive. You made me that way, too! That's why I had to get away from you." She was going to add that was why the baby had died, but no, not here, not in His presence.

But as she came closer, she saw something was wrong. The image was twisting, becoming still more distorted, as if in response to Todd's derision. For a moment, its face seemed to smirk, with its eyes spilling out of place. She fell to her knees again, whimpering.

"See?" said Todd. "Told you. It's just a fucking stain on a wall. If your Mr. Jesus ever existed, he's dead, just like I'm dead." The image continued to distort, become freakish, ugly. The crowd noticed as well, responding with catcalls and gasps.

Clare was infuriated. "Awright then, if that's what you want. Go ahead and be dead!" She rose and swung her arm around, hurling Todd's head at the wall with all her might. It smacked hard near what was left of the image's face and slid rapidly down, leaving a bloody smear and falling to the ground. There were screams, and hands grabbed her from behind.

38

JAIME AT THE SPECTACLE

Jaime walked back to the theater, distracted, thinking about death. The image of Todd's head on the sink and his headless body in the bathtub seemed burned into a part of his brain, like a picture hanging before him, about at the angle of a rearview mirror. He kept glancing and seeing it. It wasn't like he hadn't seen dead people before, he'd seen a bunch of them, mostly people in his family. The only one he'd seen before that was all bloody and gory like that was Dawnie. He hadn't seen the car actually run her over, but saw what was left of her right afterward there in the street. He didn't want that picture popping up either, so tried to think about something else.

But there was only death to think about. Like the time his cat, Nigger, got hit. He was a black cat, that's why he had that name, and scrawny. Old scary Mrs. Downey from down the street—she was dead now too but this was back when she was alive—had come ambling up across her lawn and yelled at Jaime, who was sitting in the tire swing in the backyard. "Is that your damn cat in the street?" And he ran out to the street in front of the house and there was Nigger, lying dead with his head half tore off and one of his eyeballs broken, part of it hanging about two inches out of his head. Mrs. Downey had followed him and yelled, "That cat was in my basement Tuesday night!" like it didn't matter that he was dead or that he sure wasn't going to do it again. Jaime didn't answer but turned and ran. By the time he got inside the house he was sobbing. He found Mom in the living room, sitting alone, watching one of her soap operas and drinking a beer out of a bottle like she always did. He tried to tell her about Nigger, but she acted mad too, because he was interrupting her show. "Well, you ain't gonna get another one, so shut the hell up," she'd said.

Nigger hadn't really been his cat in the first place, he just kind of lived in the garage. They didn't feed him too much or anything, though he did get into the garbage they'd put out. Jaime would bring him into the house if no one was around, which was a little hard since Nigger didn't like to be picked up, and would play with him, putting socks over his head and stuff to see him walk backward and try to get them off with his paws and his feet. Well, maybe Dawnie played with him too, but she'd do mean stuff to him, like throw him down the basement stairs, then she'd go down to find him and he'd be hiding somewhere down there. They never did figure out where he'd hide those times. When Mom noticed him in the house, she'd throw a fit. You didn't let no animals in the house where she came from, she'd say, though that was before Cheryl Sue got all fascinated with dogs, would even have them sleeping in bed with her. Jaime guessed by then, Mom didn't care anymore because she was starting to get sick. Baby wasn't allowed in the house though, he was too stinky.

When Dawnie got hit by the car, she was much more messed up than Nigger had been, but was just like him when it came to one of her eyeballs. It was torn and hanging out of her head in the same way. At least, Jaime thought that was how it was, but he wasn't sure because he'd only seen her for a couple seconds and it had been so much like a bad dream, hearing the car slam into something, followed by a brief scream and everyone running outside to find Dawnie dead and mangled in the street and the old man behind the wheel breathing hard like he couldn't stop while Bud Junior yelled at him and tried to get the locked car door open, Ma and Maamaw screaming and wailing louder than ever before. Later he thought maybe her eye wasn't really like that and he was just remembering what Nigger had looked like because that was another hit and run car accident where somebody

183

dead was left lying in the street.

At Dawnie's funeral, down in Dayville at the Hardwick Funeral Home, Jaime couldn't see how her eye was. They had to keep the coffin closed up because of her condition, they said. Ma and Cheryl Sue and old Aunt Dawn—who Dawnie was named after—and Aunt Dell and Aunt Susie and Cousin Florence and some other women relatives he didn't even know the names of were all screaming so much, like they did at Pa's funeral and Pappaw's funeral, which was right after that, but they were both in open caskets and looked like they were asleep except they weren't snoring or even breathing, just lying there, plus they were kind of shriveled looking and were all dressed up in clothes that looked real uncomfortable somehow. They screamed at Bud Junior's funeral, only they did it even more so at Dawnie's funeral because she was a little girl, Jaime supposed. Bud Junior was in a closed casket at his funeral too, and Marlon didn't even have a funeral because the Hardwicks who had the funeral home got mad at the Tales for having so many funerals they probably didn't pay much for, so that time everybody came out to the house and screamed there instead.

Jaime figured there wouldn't be all that screaming at Todd's funeral, if he had one, because the only other funeral he'd been to that wasn't for somebody in his family was for Clare's father, Mr. Hardwick, also down at the Hardwick Funeral Home, and that was really quiet though a lot of people were there. Some were relatives, but not many Jaime really knew, and the Tales didn't stay very long. Maamaw said she wanted to go to pay her respects and to sign the guestbook, but Mom didn't act like she even wanted to go. Clare was there and had dark circles around her eyes like somebody'd hit her, but she didn't cry or say anything at all while they were there. Funny, because with Todd, when she found his head and all, she acted more like people in Jaime's family, screaming and talking to the dead person and not making sense and stuff. In fact, Clare talking to Todd's head like that was pretty much the same as Aunt Dell crying and talking to the corpse in the coffin at Pappaw's funeral.

It occurred to Jaime, as cars passed him by, that Shannon might be driving around in some other car and see him. If he did and came after him, Jaime decided, he'd run, but if he was closing in on him he'd yell that he didn't have the car no more, it was parked out by Todd's house. He still wasn't going to say anything about Todd because that would be too much to yell over your shoulder while you're trying to run away, and besides, he didn't really want to get involved with the whole thing. After that thought came to him, each time he heard a car approaching he'd cringe a little, but they'd just whiz by, so apparently Shannon wasn't in any of them.

When he finally reached the movie theater, the crowd outside looked much bigger than it had before. There were at least four different TV station vans with lights and cameras next to them and people holding microphones and talking at the cameras while some people stood around watching them. An old man in a three-cornered hat like Paul Revere and with a big crudely painted banner with pictures of Jesus and stuff on it that looked like he'd made it himself was still caterwauling as he had been early that morning, but his voice was all hoarse so you couldn't understand what he was saying and nobody was paying much attention to him. There was a little group of children singing church stuff real offkey, but you couldn't make out the words to those either. Other people were laughing or yelling, though an awful lot of them, the younger people who looked like the kind who'd go to movies there, looked like they were all drunk or maybe on drugs. Some were rolling around together on the ground, not just in pairs but bunches of them, and some weren't wearing a lot of clothes, even though it was pretty chilly out. Some people standing around watching were laughing like they couldn't stop, grabbing their stomachs like they hurt, while a few other people were crying and yelling. It reminded Jaime of the time his brother Marlon got put in the state hospital after getting arrested trying to shop at the supermarket naked— "thrown in the looney bin" Maamaw had said—and they all went out to visit him, and Jaime and Dawnie had gotten separated from the others and walked around this one building there where you could hear a bunch of people inside the buildings yelling and crying. It had scared the two of them so much they'd run like crazy to get away from there.

Then Jaime saw a bunch of cops in front of the wall and they'd put up a bunch of that yellow police tape they use to keep people from getting too close to the picture of the man on the wall. Big bright lights on poles had been set up to shine on the wall. He walked near to where one of the TV people was talking excitedly into a microphone with a big TV camera pointed at her face, a real pretty woman with red hair whom he'd seen on TV before.

"—where only minutes ago a young woman hurled a severed human head at the image on the wall. Many onlookers believed it was a prank, but police have now confirmed that the severed head was indeed real. The woman was arrested on the spot, but both she and the victim remain unidentified at this time. As you at home can likely see, as we here on the scene can see plainly, a smear of blood remains on the wall directly over the image, left when the head slid down the wall after being thrown, horrifying witnesses."

Jaime walked up closer, standing behind the TV reporter and gawking at the wall. Some guy grabbed his arm and yanked him to one side, giving him a real dirty look. He must have been too close to the reporter and visible on TV. He walked around to another spot, right by the police tape, where he could still see. The blood smear was a faint, uneven line running down from the area near the figure's head, reminding him of a shit-stain in underpants. That, in turn, brought a realization: the wall was right below where his apartment was. Could the image have maybe come from all that backed-up poop that disappeared from the toilet when he was pumping it with the plunger? *Uh-oh.*

He was dazed, and his chest started hurting again. The picture, maybe just a big poop stain from the toilet in his apartment he wasn't supposed to be living in. And a woman threw a head at it. It must have been Clare with Todd's head. Now Jaime was worried he might get in some bad trouble over this stuff.

At that scary thought, as if provoked by it, it began to rain, really hard. A groan went up from some in the crowd. "Wash it away, Lord!" someone called out, and Jaime wondered whether they meant the blood smear or the other one. In fact, the rain was slanted so it hit the image directly, as if it were aimed in that way. It did seem to be having an effect on not only the blood but the human-like image as well, which began to shift, as if morphing slowly. What appeared to be its belly swelled while its legs thinned and twisted inward.

Jaime decided to look around the opposite side of the building, to where the fire escape was that he used to get in and out of what he thought of as his apartment upstairs, but some guys in yellow helmets and some kind of uniform were on the fire escape, talking and pointing upward. Maybe they had figured something out about the source of the image on the wall. With a sinking feeling, he stepped back around to the side where the image was, and as he did, a great moan went up from the crowd.

He saw why when he looked again at the image. It was still changing and far more rapidly than before. Its head and upward arm became freakishly thicker, and the arm sprouted a lump that elongated quickly. "Look, now he's giving us the finger!" someone shouted, and that was followed by more groans and some wailing and loud, if muddled, appeals to the Lord, accompanied by bursts of delighted laughter. "I'm melting, I'm melting!" someone shrieked in plain imitation of the Wicked Witch of the West. A lone voice began to chant ,"No rain, no rain!" and one or two others chimed in, but the effort soon died away. Meanwhile, the image continued to shift, now shrinking into a formless blob. There was much lamenting, and the laughter seemed to fall silent.

By this time Jaime had to pee pretty badly—perhaps the rain itself had brought that need to the forefront of his mind—and walked around to the far side of the building, past the front, where police cars and fire engines with flashing lights were parked. He thought he might find an isolated section of wall there to pee against, since there were a lot of weeds growing there and there wasn't room for people to stand around. As it happened, the area around that wall was empty of people. He hurried up to it, pulled out his dick and began to pee. While doing so, he noticed a window at the very bottom of the wall that appeared to be open a bit. Walking over and pulling at it, it came open easily. And it was wide enough for him to squeeze through . . .

39

MEG AND HER FRIENDS IN THE CAR

"They just gave you this car?" Tyler was holding on to the edges of his seat like he expected the car to go off the road any minute.

"I swear," said Meg. "It was this woman. She was talking about how the world was going to end so she wouldn't need it."

"Jesus fuck," said Ryan, lounging in the back seat. "These people are so nuts. You should have seen the woman at the thing who threw the head at Jesus!"

"Omigod, yes, it was insane!" said Tyler. "She was—"

"What? She threw a head? A human head?" Meg stepped harder on the gas pedal for a moment and the car jounced in protest.

"Yes, a real head," said Ryan. "Somebody said she'd been talking to the head, too. And somebody tackled her and then the police came up and she was like having a connip—"

"The old gal who gave me this fucking car had a head with her, too!"

"You're kidding," said Ryan, shaking his dreadlocks.

"No! And she was kind of talking to it. I asked her where she got it. It looked real, almost."

"No way! That was fucking her!" Ryan sat up, grabbing the back of Meg's seat as the car jounced again. "It was real! The head!"

"What?!"

"It was a real severed head! The TV lady said!"

Meg screamed briefly and the car swerved.

"Hey, watch it! Don't get freaked out!"

"It was a real head, and I was right here in the car with her!" Megs scream was louder and more sustained than before.

"Jesus, you should have been in the screaming contest," said Ryan. "Woulda won."

"Meg, you better let me drive, okay?"

"Yeah, let Tyler drive, for Christ's sake."

"I'm fine, I just can't fucking believe it was a real head!"

"Why'd it look fake?" Ryan leaned back and pulled his legs up on the seat.

"Because you don't expect somebody to like have a real head with them."

"Not even when they give you a free car?"

"About this car, you know," said Tyler, "we'd better take it to the cops. Like, now." He leaned against Meg, touching her hand on the steering wheel.

"No way, I need a car," said Meg, elbowing hard against him. "Quit it! I'm like, fine."

40

JAIME WATCHES A MOVIE

Jaime had banged his knee when he fell from the window to the floor into the darkened basement. He limped up the stairs, hoping to make it all the way up to his apartment, if he could avoid being noticed by those men up there on the wall. He had some stuff there he wanted to get, a box with some old family photos in it he'd found in the attic at home, and a toy robot he'd had as a kid and retained an odd fondness for. At first it seemed that no one was on the first floor, but then he heard some men talking some distance away and could somehow tell from their voices they were cops. He heard footsteps, too, coming his way, as the voices became louder. He ducked into the showing room to avoid them, but as soon as he did, he almost exited when he heard more voices but these voices were different and what they said didn't make sense because they weren't speaking English. He realized a movie was being shown, though, looking around, all the seats were empty. He hoped it wasn't a scary one. He didn't really like scary movies. Plus, he was really tired.

He sat down in the back, found a sack of popcorn on a nearby

190

seat. Hungry, he picked it up and ate some. It was cold and the butter was greasy. On the screen were some anxious-looking Chinamen in suits and ties, standing under bright lights outside a building at night, kind of like what he'd seen outside, and jabbering away excitedly over something. He'd seen movies with Asians before, but not ones where they weren't talking English, though what they said usually didn't match the movements of their mouths. With this movie, words in English appeared at the bottom of the screen but went by too fast for him to read them. The music, though, was very dramatic, suggesting, he thought, the movie was almost over.

The image on the screen shifted to one of a young Chinaman digging in a woods with a shovel, frantically, finally throwing it down to grab handfuls of dirt and toss them aside, clearing off the lid of a coffin, a wooden box Jaime thought looked quite a bit like the outhouse in the woods. The young man, wild-eyed and with straight black hair standing on end, tore at the side of the box, trying to open it. As he did, a banging came from within and an eerie wailing was heard. He fell back, a terrified look on his face, and the coffin's lid flew open.

A Chinese girl leaped out and rose upward, floating some feet off the ground before him. She wore a nearly transparent white gown that flowed with the wind. Her hair was very long and red, also flowing majestically, and her eyes had no whites but were totally black, wide and shining. With a stern expression, she tore open the front of her gown, exposing a fleshless ribcage and internal organs. She reached into her chest, yanking out her bloody pulsing heart and holding it aloft.

The heart became the close-up focus of the image on the screen. It quickly grew a mouth full of long, blood-drenched fangs, the source of the unending wail. She tossed the heart upward and, in a moment, it descended and its wail became a high-pitched scream. The young Chinaman, kneeling before the floating girl on his knees and elbows, screamed along with it as the heart fell and smacked into his upturned face. Its mouth opened wide and bit savagely into the young man's cheeks, ripping the flesh off quickly and leaving more and more of his skull exposed as his own mouth continued to scream.

Fixed on the scene before him, with the music rising to a crescendo, Jaime felt a terrible pain in his chest, clutched at it as the screen and all around him went dark and silent.

41

SHANNON AND DEWEY ARGUE

"Awright, awright, that's beside the fuckin' point," said Shannon.

"The point is your wife's not stupid, man. She knows more than you think she does, I bet. That's why she's pissed. She doesn't want you to get in trouble, that's all."

"Yeah? How does she know, 'cause you told her?"

"What do you mean, I told her? When would I have told her?"

"I dunno. Sounds like something you'd do."

"Aw, c'mon, when did I ever—"

"Here you are giving me advice about my marriage. When were you ever married? When did you even hang onto a chick for more than three months or some shit?"

"Jesus. Fuck you, man," said Dewey.

"Fuck you too," said Shannon. "It's true and you know it."

Dewey was very bruised by these words but kept it hidden. "Awright, man, awright, that's enough, I'm done. I'm just saying, we're not gonna find Jaime and the car tonight. Let's give this up, awright?"

"I'm not gonna let fucking Jaime Tales make off with— What the fuck?! There it is!" The Thunderbird passed them going in the other direction. "Jesus fucking Christ!" yelled Shannon, making a u-turn and barreling after it. Dewey winced. God, why did he let Shannon drive? It was his grandma's car!

42

BENNY ON THE RUN

Benny was driving much faster than he realized, watching the road ahead of him as if it were a movie on a screen. He shouldn't have done it, wished he hadn't, was out of his head. Now he was really in trouble, worse than that time he sent that anonymous letter to Lionel's mother about how Lionel had gotten involved with a dangerous criminal with a long police record and Lionel knew right away he had written it. *A bomb threat, you could go to prison for doing that, couldn't you?* Maybe Roni didn't recognize him. She didn't say anything, but he had hung up before she could have. She probably did. He sounded like himself even to himself, but maybe she wouldn't say anything anyway. She wouldn't want to get him in trouble. They had gotten along fairly well though she could get exasperated quite easily. He could never decide whether she respected gay men or not, but Hobie seemed to like her very much. Then again, Hobie didn't like gay men either. He was kind of a self-hater. Anyway, maybe she'd sympathize with him as an individual because she'd been through some heartache too with that slimy husband of hers. He didn't know what she saw in him except he was kind of handsome in a scuzzy way. Not that that had ever appealed to Benny personally, but he could understand it. Besides, she knew how Hobie could be and how he was heading for real trouble putting that drug in those water coolers. He really should have called the police but then Hobie would have been arrested and in God knows how much trouble. Maybe calling in the bomb threat was the right thing to do to get the theater closed, not that Hobie would appreciate what he'd tried to do to help him but God knows he'd been through that before. *My God, the way these people drive. Why don't they watch where they're going for heaven's— What in the world is that? Todd Dewolf's car coming right at— Stop! No! Please! Omigod—*

43

SKY HITCHES A RIDE

S ky stood on the roadside in the small hours. When a car passed by, she watched it approach, trying to see the driver, not moving until it was close, then put out her thumb, trying to smile. Only seven cars had gone past in . . . how long? It seemed like at least an hour. Perhaps she not only was unable to smile but had a scared expression. Or maybe she looked awful. She had not looked in the mirror before fleeing from Todd's house. Since then, she'd been praying, an old habit, though she had long since lost all concept of who or what she prayed to. *Please let me get out of this awful place, this town, get far away, somewhere where I can sort this out. I have to think some more . . .*

She realized she was speaking aloud, though in a whisper. *Men, so pitiful.* She'd known so many, could manipulate them when she wished to, but didn't understand them, didn't understand herself. She still called it a mission, one of her own. She told no one. But it wasn't a mission anymore, was it? She didn't believe in anything. She went on, she knew, because it was thrilling. *Don't ask me to explain . . .* But she really was trying, hoping, to help. It was what she was made for, that part was true.

But I didn't know it could go so wrong . . .

Poor Todd on the bathroom floor in a pool of blood, his head attached to his body by a scrap of flesh, wide-eyed, already dead. *The Invisible World is ever with us, full of ghosts.* She'd seen the ritual done only once, when she was seven, at the ranch in Modesto among a crowd of Kindred, holding her mother's hand and being brave. Delbert Wingdale was there. It was before Daddy Dickey and love bombing. It was a rite, he'd said, a separation of the mind and body. A gift from the Space Brothers. And it was a secret. Todd had nearly de-brained himself with the shotgun. Frantic and blind with tears, she'd completed the task, driven to do so. Possessed.

Maybe that was the answer to everything. She was possessed.

A black car approached, and she put out her thumb, not smiling but pleading with her eyes. The car slowed and stopped. A man, alone, was driving. Of course.

"Don't you know you shouldn't hitchhike? A lovely girl like you?" the driver said, turning on the ceiling light in his car. He was clean-shaven, had blond hair in a widow's peak, somehow an unpleasant face. He was grinning almost like the mask that represents comedy, taking in the sight of her.

"I probably shouldn't, but I'll have to trust you." She was too shaken to make eye contact. She got in, pulled the door closed. "Too late now," he said, and she forced a laugh.

The car started moving. He was driving rather fast.

"I don't think you're from around here, are you?"

"No."

"Just passing through, eh?"

"Umm-hmm. If you could let me out somewhere near the highway, that'd be fine."

He threw back his head and laughed, too loud and too abruptly. "You know what's odd?"

"What?"

"I smell blood."

Smell? A chill ran through her. "Oh, yes, I guess I cut myself."

"You have blood on your dress, too. And your eye is bruised, isn't it?" He winced a bit, peering at her. The ceiling light was still on. She wished he'd turn it off.

"Is it? I didn't know."

"Sounds like you've had a bad night already."

They often said strange things. Besides, she was upset. Her perceptions could be off. Maybe he wasn't driving as fast as it seemed, wasn't too often studying her rather than watching the road and with a disturbingly hungry gaze. She felt nothing for him, couldn't tease, couldn't even try.

Her prayers began again, silently now. *Please let me get through this ride. Let me live. Let me go on with my mission, and please don't let it be in vain.*

ACKNOWLEDGMENTS

Thanks to Andersen Prunty and C.V. Hunt for emergency editorial assistance.

ABOUT THE AUTHOR

Pete Risley is also the author of *Rabid Child* (New Pulp Press, 2010), *The Toehead* (N.H.N.T., 2016), and *Office Mutant* (Grindhouse Press, 2018). He lives in Columbus, Ohio and is a distant cousin of Gelett Burgess, author of the celebrated poem *The Purple Cow: Reflections on a Mythic Beast Who's Quite Remarkable, at Least.*

Other Grindhouse Press Titles

Prunty

Made in USA - Kendallville, IN
1186894_9781941918845
10.28.2020 0839